The Universe

Mike Matzdorff

THE UNIVERSE

Published by Green Crow Publishing, LLC
www.greencrowpublishing.com

ISBN: 978-1-967309-00-9 (ebook)
ISBN: 978-1-967309-01-6 (paperback)
ISBN: 978-1-967309-02-3 (audiobook)

First Edition: June 10, 2025

0 9 8 7 6 5 4 3 2 1

Praise for The Universe

"Complex, high-concept, and beautifully rendered —tactile in its specificity. A magical piece of material, coming at a time when the world needs it most! Who knew so much could be revealed in just a couple hundred pages?"

— **Darren Stein,** Writer & Director of
Jawbreaker

"How many times have you heard the saying, 'The Universe Works in Mysterious Ways'? Well, in Mike Matzdorff's first novel *The Universe*, you find out the Universe is even more mysterious than you can possibly imagine. *The Universe* is a unique and entertaining page-turner that keeps finding imaginative twists and fresh, new ways keep you guessing from cover to cover. Matzdorff creates an original 'world behind the world we know' that makes you wonder just how much you REALLY want to know about how the Universe works!"

— **John D. Beck,** Executive Producer of
Fuller House

"If you were ever hoping to unravel the mystery of the Universe, this book will do it. But first it will mix pathos, intrigue, the past, office jobs, and the human condition into a swirling cauldron of mind-bending and metaphysical storytelling that is simultaneously fantastical and relatable and will help you worry a little less about your own universe in the grand scheme of things."

— **Carlos Kotkin**, 14-time *Moth* Short Story Prize winner

"A mind-bendingly original debut. Unpredictable, thought provoking and at times wildly funny, Matzdorff's prose will stick in your brain for weeks after. You'll never look at our 'normal' world the same way again."

— **Ted Caplan**, Co-author of *Unpregnant*

"Our lives unfold in infinite and unexpected ways. However, Matzdorff creates for us a more knowable Universe—one that's actually run out of an office in Queens. While an easy read, it explores the march of history, the challenges of loss, and the purpose of existence, all while navigating absurd twists that ultimately remind us not to take life too seriously."

— **Matt Walsh**, Actor on *Veep*

For Peter and Sherry.
It would have been impossible without you.

there are mysteries
in the Universe

Prologue

JULY 1624
Rome

IT's a hot night in Rome. Difficult to say how hot because thermometers wouldn't be invented until the late 1600s. The Viae Romanae (streets and alleyways) of the city are empty. The scent of flowers and sleeping oxen drifts through the air. Candles flicker here and there in open windows. Wisps of smoke drift skyward.

The full moon is perched behind the Obelisk in Saint Peter's Square. A young woman in a hooded cape hurries through its shadow. She turns down a narrow alleyway, cautiously carrying a package. Her foot finds a loose brick in the deserted street. She steadies herself. The package starts to cry.

"Ich werde auf dich aufpassen, Junge," she whispers in German to the boy. "Deine Mutter war wie meine Schwester. Das ist sicherlich das, was das Universum von mir verlangt. Du bist jetzt frei."

Her words are meant to soothe the child. *Your mother*

1

was like my sister. You're free now. The wavering in her voice could go either way. But how would an infant know the difference between panic, fear, or tragedy? Or why they are together at this moment?

Rounding a corner, she halts at the sight of something. A handwritten note, in German. It's stuck to a stone wall in front of her. Surprise at such a thing, in the 17th-century Papal States on the Italian Peninsula, is an understatement. At the top of the page is a small black square with a blue circle painted in its center. Below that, beautiful German script fills the light brown sheet. She reads. It's written as a six line poem, and seems specifically for her—the third line is an offer, mixed with a threat—*"Wirst du dich gesellen, oder wird deine Buße bezahlt?"* But from whom?

Her gaze reaches the bottom of the page and the breath leaves her lungs as she reads her own name.

Her quivering hand carefully removes the fragile papyrus from the wall. She clutches it to her chest and rushes off into the night.

Long Island

A WEATHERED, wood-paneled 1989 Jeep Grand Wagoneer drives north on Kirkup Lane. Maple and elm trees sway in the soft September wind. Cattails grow in bunches here and there along the side of the lane. Morning birdsong and insect buzz play as the background track of this peaceful countryside setting.

This part of Long Island, New York is a mix of rural, agricultural, and vineyard land. The locals don't mind the tourists, but they don't love them either.

The Wagoneer pulls up to the stop sign at Kirkup and State Route 48. Katie is at the wheel. Her fair complexion, inherited from her European roots, shows against her brown shoulder-length hair, tousled from the breeze through the open window. She wears expensive sunglasses and a worn t-shirt.

The t-shirt belongs to her husband, John. He sits in the passenger seat, sketching on the back side of a postcard. He looks out into the young sunrise. It's early, and a few colorful clouds remain. John never misses a chance to stop and smell the roses—or look at the colorful morning clouds, in this case.

In a moment, they'll lose their rosy orange tones and reduce to plain white, puffy cumulus clouds.

Meet the Paulson's. Early forties, no kids and big dreams. City dwellers with country aspirations.

"You want me to drive?" John asks.

"I want to get home sooner than later," Katie says, "and keep working on the pitch."

He knows the answer before he asks the question, but he asks it anyway. "Are you excited about it?"

Excited? That is too strong a word for how Katie feels. She has spent two decades in a career where her highest achievements involve getting approvals from fresh college graduates—graduates who have slid their way into the machine of modern corporate life. Who think everything is in service of the company and about the bottom line.

Only life experience can teach otherwise, and living in this corporate universe for twenty years has revealed this to Katie. John knew all along. She has learned the importance of finding and living her truth, despite the world insisting on what's best.

"I'm excited for it to be done," she says.

"I think we're ready," he says without looking up from his sketch.

"It's Park Avenue, John. We can't be too prepared for that fuckin' crowd. We'll sign the final agreement, collect the check, and be back out here by Thanksgiving." She shifts in her seat and takes a drink of lukewarm coffee. "I'm ready to return to making some meaningful art and slip a toe into the corporate world to keep us funded and them entertained. I'm tired of this—it feels like too much work."

He holds up the postcard. "Look." It's a sketch of the

two of them in a rowboat on a lake, among the cattails and the clouds. He is an absolute whiz with a pencil. "We're in the same boat—get it?"

Despite the terrible pun, this is on the list of *why they are so perfect together*. Katie knows she has some sharp edges, and he knows how to take the edge off. It's been like this from the start.

"We *are* in the same boat. My love, you are a talent." She leans over and offers her cheek, keeping her eyes on the road. He accepts the offer with a kiss.

"I'll save it for you." He tucks the postcard up into the sun visor.

They are westbound. The morning sun is behind them and reflects off of a sign on the roadside that simply reads "CAFE."

"Pie?" he asks.

"It's a little early for pie, isn't it?"

"Never too early for pie. I'll say good morning to Ruby for you."

"I can't believe that chihuahua is still alive, it must be twenty."

Katie waits, engine running, radio off. Through the front window of the cafe, she sees John, a to-go container in one hand and a plastic fork in the other, laughing with the retiree behind the counter. He glances at her. She raises her eyebrows and signals him to hurry up, her index finger extended and swirling in a circle.

A few minutes later back in the Jeep, John feeds a bite of rhubarb pie to Katie. "You were right," she says with a full mouth, "not too early for pie. It's always perfect. How is Ruby?"

He takes a bite. "Ruby has walked over the Rainbow Bridge."

"No."

"Afraid so."

Nothing lasts forever.

Along the state road, which they have driven countless times together, and that Katie has traversed her entire life, the trees are starting to hint at the change of seasons. Some yellows, some reds, some leaves floating down.

One leaf lodges itself on the windshield, then blows away. Katie smiles at this as John sleeps in the passenger seat, some pie filling stuck on the corner of his mouth.

"I love you John Paulson," she whispers. "You're the best thing that has ever happened to me."

She loves his face, and his manner, and his entire being. He is Yin to her Yang. Chocolate to her peanut butter.

"I love you too," he whispers and licks the pie filling from his face.

She grunts at him for being awake, aggravated. "Faker!"

she says. It's not real aggravation, though—it's playful. He knows it, and she knows it.

We all do. And what she said is true, awake or not. They both feel lucky to have found each other. It's an extraordinary thing to find the right person, someone who fits, someone who makes it easy to be who you are—and they have.

After a couple hours, the country road is replaced by the interstate. The swaying trees by row houses and low apartment buildings. Ahead, in the distance, is the Manhattan skyline.

Quebec

NINETEEN YEARS ago in mid-November near Belval, Quebec, the farmers woke up to three inches of snow.

The main roads were plowed and salted overnight. At 7:15 in the morning, some of the smaller roads are still works in progress.

A stake-bed Ford idles outside a breakfast restaurant. A cigarette burns, balanced on the side mirror outside the truck. The driver is inside getting a coffee to-go.

The truck is loaded with boxes of maple syrup and crates of small animals, destined for the restaurants of Quebec City. The cages have square tin signs attached to them with wires: "Poulet/Chicken," "Lapin/Rabbit," "Pigeonneau/Squab." Except for the chickens, the animals are huddled together for warmth, some with their eyes closed.

A rope is tied across the back of the open stake bed, and then it isn't. A woman's gloved hand loosens the knot.

The driver, cigarette in one hand and coffee in the other, chugs down an unplowed country road. The chickens peck at each other and cluck as they watch the cage with the rabbits inch past the loose rope and gently slide, unharmed, onto the snow-covered road. The driver, unaware, takes a drag off the cigarette and turns up the morning news report on the radio.

About an hour later, the morning news has an update: a charter bus from New York, on its way to a winery tour, slid off the road. "There were a couple dozen rabbits right in the middle of the road," the driver says to the reporter on the scene.

The driver had swerved to avoid the rabbits, and the bus skidded off the snowy road into a ditch in response. The impact knocked out most of the windows on one side of the bus. There were no fatalities, human or rabbit, but a few elderly members of the tour had to be taken to local medical facilities. They received treatment for bumps, bruises, and exposure to the elements.

A couple from New York City, because of the cold temperature, contracts pneumonia soon after.

At the time of the accident, Katie, an overachieving student at the prestigious Rhode Island School of Design, is summoned by the school's office and informed that her parents have been in a bus accident. She is given emotional support, the option to postpone her final exams of the term, and the phone number of the Canadian hospital.

Katie collects her parents and two bottles of prescription antibiotics. Her mother dies of severe pneumonia on Christmas Eve, and her father follows twenty days later.

New York City

THERE's nothing quite like New York City in autumn. The brutal heaviness of summer is gone. The icy chill of January lurks, ignored on the horizon. A passenger ferry navigates the East River. The downtown A train rumbles past. The windows of a hospital reflect the evening sun. The city is alive. In the West Village, scooters weave through traffic with groceries and takeout. Traffic lights seem irrelevant to them. Young children walk gleefully with their parents, chasing falling leaves. They kick and stomp, hoping for a good crunch.

On West 4th Street, there's an awkward intersection that was clearly designed for horse and carriage. The sidewalk and cobblestones have buckled, thanks to an ancient silver maple tree whose grandeur fills the corner. Under the maple tree, there's an out-of-the-way bistro that has been generously allowed to share its space.

In the buzzing dining room, the food and the people glow. (Money well-spent on good lighting.) Conversation and the sound of a well-oiled restaurant fill the room. Hustle, bustle, forks, glasses, and laughter. A table of old friends gather at a prime spot for people-watching and access to the bar. This group has occupied this same table every third Thursday for the past decade.

"Katie, I hear you guys are thinking about kids again, maybe?"

Six sets of eyes smile and cautiously await a reaction.

Katie and John are the last of this tight-knit group to be childless. She is a career woman. He is known for his pencil, his puns, and his lightheartedness and patience. They have talked about kids, saved for kids, and endured inquiries from relatives. Both had parents who started late in life. For the last ten years, they've discussed how they didn't want to repeat that mistake. Young parents have more energy. Young parents aren't as heavily invested in their careers. Young parents don't enter a contest, win a three-day winter wine and cheese tour in Quebec, slide off the road due to a spilled crate of rabbits, develop severe pneumonia, and die within three weeks of each other while their child is away at college.

"We're thinking about it," John says.

"He's thinking about it," Katie says. She kisses him tenderly and raises her glass of red. "Here's to big thinkers—and my beautiful man. If tomorrow goes well, then we will talk seriously about kids. Wish me luck." They do. "Cheers."

Katie quietly waves over the server. "I'll take the check when it's time." He nods. She occasionally likes to affirm the pecking order in this group and turns up one corner of her mouth to John.

Apartment 4F

JOHN CLOSES the door to Apartment 4F and twists the top lock. This is home. It's exactly as they want it. Comfortable, uncluttered, only containing what they need to feel complete and not a stitch more. Katie had the good sense to get her name onto the lease when she was twenty-one and took over the apartment after the pneumonia tragedy.

It has had a few fresh coats of paint over the years. Katie rented a sander and refinished the floors herself. Her mother had always wanted it done, and her father had always promised to do it. But time caught them—and really, her father was long on promises and short on action.

Although it was Katie's childhood home, she had no attachment to the contents—only disdain. She is a doer, always has been. To her, the unread books, unfinished projects and mismatched sets of thrift store linens and dishes had represented a life poorly lived. Katie wanted a different life. From the age of eight, she wanted to be in business. She planned to put herself in a position of power and make her world hers. Katie's lemonade stand did well.

When she and John took over the apartment, she

completely emptied it out. Much was donated to charity or sent back to the thrift store it had come from. Some things were offered up to relatives, or to friends, and the rest was trashed. Katie only kept one thing her parents had given her. It sits in a storage unit along with their Jeep and other possessions they want to keep for their kids and for their country house, if they ever attain those things.

"I want you to know, it's okay if we don't have kids."

Katie had never heard this from him before. Always the opposite. Not pressure, just eager hope, support, warmth.

"It's okay— you can just tell me. Safe space, Kate. We can be the old people who travel and visit our friend's kids and grandkids. We'll give the best presents and take fun vacations. We can babysit, and drive them to Coney Island." He smiles. "We can go on that Rhine River cruise. Take pictures of the European countryside in matching Hawaiian shirts. It'll be fun."

She has to smile. "Hawaiian shirts...."

"Either way, I'm yours for life. We're a team. Go to that meeting tomorrow, collect the golden egg you've earned for your years of service, and move into the corner office at the lake house. I'll finish my great American novel—a kept man and starving artist."

"Your starving art landed us this deal, don't be modest."

She sets down her drink and straddles him on the couch. "My love, tomorrow night, after I close this deal and we achieve financial nirvana, we are going to get busy, break out the Twinkies, and make that baby. I'm ready."

The Boardroom

When the call came six months ago, Katie was skeptical about the sudden interest from a prominent Park Avenue corporate design firm. They requested a meeting and made a compelling pitch to acquire the business Katie and John had built. The financial upside sounded great. They sought the credibility of independent artisans, while John and Katie desired a different life. After six months of courtship, it's finally here. She and John have put together the transition plan, and today is the day all their efforts will pay off. All their hopes will be realized—an ideal scenario.

They will be remote consultants. They will review any marketing and artistic decisions. They will also spice up ad copy and keep sales materials grounded. Katie and John have a knack for making things feel friendly and organic, and that tone is in high demand in this age of aggressive selling. Make people feel at home, and then get them to subscribe to some service they will barely use.

Once the consultancy is up and running, they will move out of the city—one of John's dreams—to a house way out on Long Island that Katie's grandparents left them. They'll become avid gardeners, weekend fishing experts, leaf rakers, and set up for a long, leisurely retirement at forty-three.

"Sixth Avenue and 40th," Katie says to the taxi driver. The cab smells of curry and pine. She cracks a window. The city seems to be slowing her down today. Double-parked delivery vans, red lights, bike messengers, and potholes. "All good," she whispers, closing her eyes. She takes a minute to envision the meeting (deep inhale). This is the inevitable result and the hard-earned, blissful future (exhale). The cabbie doesn't say a word as she exits. She has him stop the car a few blocks from her eventual destination.

The glass high-rise across Bryant Park looks a little smaller from here. Less imposing. She will shed her usual pre-meeting jitters with a walk through the park. The little green havens dotting New York City always bring her calm. Black coffee from the corner shop, a ten-minute walk, and some deep breaths will do the trick.

Approaching the building, Katie sees two window washers in blue jumpsuits dealing with a broken pulley system. *Terrifying job*, she thinks. It takes thirty seconds to get around them, through the revolving door, and into the lobby. "Twenty-four," she says with a nod to the person at the desk. The security guard points up without looking at Katie. Katie tosses her half cup of coffee into the bin and pushes the silver circle marked 24.

The view from the boardroom is breathtaking. A wall of glass looks to the west, and the city sprawls out beneath them. Eleven people sit around a long oval conference table listening to Katie talk. "...and the reduction of the overhead of 'in-office' work will boost our productivity and lower costs in the long term. With the plan we have outlined— that's page seven on the handout—remote cooperation and the online client participation engine will pay for itself in three to four years and essentially be 'no cost' after that. Presuming consistent production levels."

Katie hates "corporate speak." But this is the language of today's executives, and she had to work it into her plan. It's a necessary evil in this business.

At the far end of the table, the person in charge, a buttoned-down woman in her early thirties, thanks Katie for her words and initiates a round of gratuitous applause. "What an exciting opportunity this has turned into, and Katie—such a great preso," the exec says. "We do have some news to share, and now seems like a good time, really the best possible time to share. Are you open to that?"

"Of course." This is off-script, in Katie's mind. "Please."

"Thank you so much. Well, as of two days ago, corporate came up with a very exciting plan for growth, and as always with growth, some pruning is necessary," she says. "Unfortunately, due to the challenging times and a new direction for not just us but all the divisions under the umbrella of our parent company...."

The speech drones on, skirting any frank delivery of bad news and using the most evasive language possible. Katie hears the words "downsizing" and "evaluating new future possibilities."

"Excuse me?"

"I said, we are really excited about inviting you to evaluate new future possibilities—outside of our agreement. We will be exercising Clause B under Section Four to postpone our forward motion for an undetermined time, due to our evaluation of how artificial intelligence impacts output and creative needs. Your cooperation is greatly appreci—"

"Now, what the fuck is this all about?!" Katie bursts from her seat. "You've got to be kidding me. You're putting us on the shelf? Undetermined time? AI? We gave you our life's work!"

The woman stands, "And we appreciate that. We—"

"Shut the hell up, Irene! I'd like to 'invite' you to get your lawyers ready to evaluate your future lawsuit."

After Katie bangs through the door, the silence is deafening.

* * *

Work never comes home. That was part of their wedding vows, and it isn't going to start now. John will ask how it went. She will calmly say it was a "worst case scenario nightmare shitstorm." They can talk about it tomorrow during their ritual morning coffee walk. Done and done.

Inhale—and she opens the door marked 4F.

"Congratulations!" John and their six closest friends announce. (All the attendees of the previous evening's meal.) In tandem with the yelp of congratulations, mini party poppers burst with confetti and the smell of a cap gun.

Less than sixty seconds later, John closes the door behind the last departing guest.

"Are you going to want your 'congratulations' gift?" He holds out a small terracotta pot with daisies growing in it.

"Yeah." She takes the token and strokes the delicate white petals.

These two know how to read each other. It's part of their greatness. John takes his turn to receive whatever she needs to unload.

"You want to talk about it?"

"No, not here. Rules are rules."

"Rules can be broken. How bad?"

She picks up some of the confetti from the poppers. "As bad as you could imagine." The pink paper coils halfway to the floor. "I'm going to call the attorneys in the morning, after I'm done being furious. I mean, how much time did we spend with this, John? They rambled on about growth and pruning and downsizing and different directions—without saying an *actual—fucking—thing*. What balls—a different direction?! They will crash and burn, good riddance."

"Maybe there's a grand plan or something. A plan that's not for the corporate douchebags. It's for us, the little guys who make all the beautiful things. It'll turn out to be a good thing. You'll see." He kisses her, and tugs gently on her earlobes. His smile and his calm are some of the reasons she fell in love with him in the first place. "Everything happens for a reason."

"The reason must be that I am supposed to sue those assholes for stringing us along and screwing with *my* grand plan."

"Things find a way to work themselves out, Kate. Let's take a day off and have another look."

She knows he's right.

"Drink?" John asks. He's got her usual Old Fashioned ready. She's only now noticing the candles he lit. There's a Twinkie cut in half on the table. He knows all of her favorite things.

"At least I still have you." She embraces him deeply.

"When the Universe gives you lemons...."

"I love it when you get philosophical."

The Old Fashioned is gone in a swig. She feeds him half of the Twinkie, and then rubs some of the cream filling on her neck, before shoving the rest into her mouth. "Come here," she orders. They aren't newlyweds, but nothing has changed for them.

John kisses her then asks under his breath, "Do you want to call me Irene?"

"Maybe later," she says.

Their clothes hit the floor. The height of passion. These are lovers who know each other well. A neighbor bangs on the wall, Katie laughs and looks at him—something is wrong. His face is pale, he's cold, sweat beads on his forehead. He's trying to say something—his lips open, but no words, just a grating, gurgling sound. "John! No!"

The neighbor bangs again on the wall.

She shakes him. "HELP!" His eyes roll back in his head. He twitches and drools. She tries to shake him out of it.

911 is on the way.

In the back of the ambulance, Katie holds John's hand. They bounce over a pothole. Sirens wail. He's cold. His eyelids flutter. Katie glances forward. The driver is drinking a soda. She strokes John's hair. "You're going to be fine." She has no idea how true that might be. "You're starting to look better, I'm here."

The corridors at Lenox Health on 7th Avenue are buzzing. Katie paces. Her arms folded, a tear-stained face. Every time a door opens, her eyes dart in its direction. A doctor pushes through the doors from the emergency room, and their eyes meet. He approaches her slowly; he's visibly tired. "Is he going to be okay? What was it?"

The change in the doctor's face is slight, but sad. He puts a warm hand on her shoulder. "We did everything we could. I'm sorry." Everything after that is a blur.

The Hologram

THE PIXELATED HOLOGRAM stands about twenty feet tall. The imagery fades toward the edges. It's semi-transparent, and behind it, pinpoint lights pulse here and there. The pinpoint lights recede, their vanishing points deep in a black void of indeterminate size.

The hologram is a sailing ship with three masts and a full rig of sails. It pushes with force through a storm, big waves. Lightning cracks in the distance. On the bottom left in the faded edge of the hologram is a four-digit number: 1654.

"Stop there," a voice says. "Show me the deck." The hologram freezes.

"Of course." The keyboard clicks.

The view changes. A surly sea sprays mist across the deck. Two sailors, their clothes and skin filthy, their eyes desperate as they are devious, have hold of a bound man. Rope wraps around his arms and chest, around his knees, and down to his ankles.

A young girl of twelve or thirteen, with the face of a child and the body of a woman, is being held by a third sailor. She has brown skin, sharp features, and terrified blue eyes. Blood collects in the corner of her mouth. Her clothes are torn to a point of immodesty.

"*Don Gabriel, please...,*" the bound man cries out in Spanish, "*por favor, ella es una niña. Ella ya perdió a su madre y el universo nunca sería tan cruel como para dejarla huérfana.*"

"*En América habrá una nueva vida,*" the man in charge says.

"Don't leave her an orphan, it will be a new life in America," says the person watching the hologram. "New life indeed. That man is an animal."

The man in charge paces around the captive, as if on a Sunday stroll. The long, thin blade he drags across the sea-soaked deck scrapes a metallic tune. The young girl chokes with fear. "*Ninguno de nosotros quiere vivir demasiado tiempo.*"

With the words, "*None of us want to live too long,*" he rests the blade on the captive's neck. His eyes meet those of the young girl. "*Dile adiós a tu padre y hola a tu marido.*"

"Nice touch," the voice says. "Say *au revoir* to papa and hello to your husband."

"Good-bye father," says the keyboard operator.

He pulls the blade across the bound man's throat and shoves him overboard. The sea takes only a moment to consume him. His daughter is now chattel.

"She should have killed him when she had the chance."

"We have a Plan B; that's better than no plan at all."

Keep Moving

THE WOMAN TAKES twenty-nine days to travel from Rome to the Via Claudia Augusta, a road that leads north through the Alps and along the Danube to the Germanic regions. She travels by foot until she negotiates a ride on an ox cart leading a small goat herd.

She didn't expect the child to be so hungry. The boy has a voracious appetite, and his mother is dead. He won't remember her, of course; he is just one year old. He survives on blackberries found on the roadside and goat's milk.

She explains to her family how this has come to be. They welcome the boy, thinking he can be raised as a servant, perhaps.

A few days after her return, a letter is found at the door of her family's home. It bears the same mark as the one she found on the wall in Rome. She compares the writing. It looks to be in the same hand. It has only two words: *"Await instructions."* Soon, instructions arrive. The messages have tasks for her. Tasks that start simply: buy some bread and give it away to a particular person at a particular place, ask for directions from a stranger. She wonders how anyone could know when a particular person would be in a particular place. Then, every twelve to fourteen days, she finds messages upon waking. They are written in the same hand as the other notes she received. There is no answer as to where they come from.

Soon, the tasks become more complex and curious: write a letter, lock a door, kill a small animal, set a fire.

In Augsburg, a stable burns, and animals are trapped and killed. A farmer trying to save his property is badly injured. She had set the fire. Will there be consequences? The woman doesn't want to find out. She and the boy disappear—she feels the need to hide.

Her parents weep. They had come to love the boy; he laughs a lot, and they miss his laughter.

Even though she and the boy leave Augsburg, the messages follow them. They settle in Paris, where she learns French and becomes a chambermaid. People begin to ask questions about them. The woman concocts a story about the boy being an African prince who she has to protect during an uprising in his country. The French are very involved in Africa and admire the boy's dark skin.

The woman and the boy settle in a quiet corner of a bustling Paris for a year. The boy grows, but not as fast as the woman imagines he should.

The letters begin coming in French. She speaks French and German to the boy, writing letters and words for him. He learns to count. She is his teacher and protector.

The letters and tasks seem important. She binds the small slips of paper with a long string, untying and retying them when new tasks arrive.

Will they ever stop?

She explores the markets and the shops. She hears other tongues from other immigrants who are escaping tyranny or poverty. Where else in the world may she find herself? She listens and asks questions. She learns bits of their languages and tastes their food. *These are good things to know*, she thinks. Customs, words, stories. She begins to learn English.

Will the messages ever stop?

One night, with candles burning in her rented room on the second floor of a building near Notre Dame, she looks out her lone window at the narrow alley below. Rats and prostitutes are its most common inhabitants.

What had she agreed to?

String-bound stacks of tasks are wrapped in cloth under her bed. She removes them and brushes off bits of disintegrated straw that had fallen from her thin mattress. She unbinds what she knows to be the very first stack of letters. Perhaps inside would be the answers to her many questions. Scores of letters, each with the same black square and blue circle, bring back memories. What will be the consequences of each action? Finally, she finds the original document, pulled from an alleyway in Rome, yellowed, cracked, and brittle.

She translates the six-line verse into English:

"The debt repaid awaits another life,
Look to the future, where souls may be saved.
Wilt thou join, or shall thy penance be paid?
You will enjoy a long and fruitful life.
When all is even, thou shalt know the time,
Embrace the Universe; the world shall change."

She accepted the invitation. She knew she must at the moment she read it. She has lived beyond her years, no question about it.

The text contains yet-unfulfilled promises—saving lives, seeing the future. How will she know when the debt is settled?

There is no one to ask these questions to; no sender was identified. Only messages and tasks: stop a stranger and ask for directions, leave a door open, talk to a peasant, steal some meat and give it to an old woman's dog.

It may never end. The fruitful life is too long delayed.

Enough is enough, she decides. *No more tasks.*

Thomasine Osborne

1651
Calais, France

CROSSING the English Channel in the 17th century is no easy task. A voyage in June of 1651, the return of the Osborne family from a two-year stint in France, happens at an inopportune time.

A young woman, Thomasine Osborne, has been privately schooling in Paris at her mother's urging, during which time her mother hires a retired Sorbonne professor, Pierre Gassendi, to teach her philosophy and science. (This is only a few years before Gassendi's death.) Meanwhile, her father works for a shipping company finding ways to trade with the "New World."

Thomasine is very interested in astronomy, fascinated with the night sky and the infinite darkness beyond what is known to man. She has read Galileo's *Starry Messenger* and heard of his torment by the Catholic Church. The Osborne's are not Catholic, but, like most English, are members of the Church of England. Professor Gassendi privately doesn't care about such things; he is a scientist, and he appreciates this young woman's mind. She reminds him of his own granddaughter. The professor tells the family that, in a few years, in 1654, Thomasine should return in mid-August to see a solar eclipse. "One of the marvels of the Universe," he tells her. And so the date is entered into Thomasine's diary, and with excitement she plans for the return trip.

She begins writing to Isabelle, Gassendi's granddaughter. They become close. They are pleased that, despite different cultures and customs, they share a love of the night sky.

On a desk in a modest apartment in Paris, whose lone window looks to an alleyway occupied by rats and prostitutes, sits an envelope. There is a date and a location on the envelope. Inside is a handwritten invitation. The noted German scientist Maria Cunitz will be in Paris, giving a lecture on celestial mechanics and astronomy. She will be speaking to female students in an effort to generate equality in the scientific disciplines. "All the great minds are not men," she had said in a published interview. She, in fact, is one of the reasons Thomasine's family is in Paris.

The lecture will occur on the same day the Osborne's are to return to England.

The envelope would be delivered to Professor Gassendi, who would in turn share it with Mrs. Osborne, who would insist that her husband delay the trip to England. "Just for one day...," she would say.

Thomasine would have arrived at one of the smaller lecture halls at the Sorbonne (even the brilliant Maria Cunitz could not fill the Grand Amphithéâtre de la Sorbonne) to find the doors closed, the hall empty, and no Maria Cunitz. The invitation is meant to be a ruse.

But the woman (and the boy) have had enough. No more tasks. The woman wants to live out her life quietly in Paris; however, the Universe has other plans.

Because the envelope containing the invitation is not delivered, the trip to England is not delayed. Only a month later, because of this, Thomasine Osborne is introduced to Thomas Parris. They are religiously compatible, culturally compatible, and of age to begin a family. They marry and soon after are blessed with a son.

They don't know that the son will be responsible for the death of twenty people across an ocean years later.

Their son, Samuel Parris, becomes a landowner, a slave owner, a Harvard graduate, and a minister. He goes into the ministry more for financial stability than for his proximity to godliness. He is responsible for the Salem Witch Trials, the murder of twenty, and broken family lines, which present their own sets of future complications in the Universe.

An Empty Home

THE HALL LIGHT is still on in Katie and John's West Village apartment. It is as she left it. Two whiskey glasses and a bottle of Dalmore scotch stand on the kitchen counter.

The potted daisies John had given her look thirsty; they smell of earth. She rinses out one of the whiskey glasses and uses it to give them a drink.

For Katie, walking through the apartment is a new experience. She has never lived alone there. Each room feels different. *What should I do with his toothbrush?* she thinks. His empty water glass is on a bedside table. A sketch of a bird's nest outside their window, in reality long abandoned, but in the unfinished drawing, a young mother feeds her babies a spider. The spider has a comical look on his face and is trying to push away from the gaping mouths.

Katie looks out the window next to his desk to confirm the nest is still there. A single sparrow stands in the nest, adjusting bits of straw, string, and feathers left by a previous tenant. *Moving in*, Katie thinks. The sky beyond the tree is the color of spent charcoal, heavy with dark clouds.

She bounces from room to room. Time feels like it's crawling, or even stopped. Half of the life in this place has vanished, gone forever. Katie picks up the wrapper from the Twinkie and breaks down in tears.

* * *

Over the next week, flowers and cards come. Food and drink are delivered at regular intervals. The odd, tedious items that come with dying—removing names from bank accounts, mailing death certificates, filling in insurance forms—are many. She orders ten copies of his death certificate. Everybody seems to need one to remove his name from one of their accounts.

Nine days later, on a brisk November morning, a small group gathers on a hillside at Calvary Cemetery in Queens. Katie has asked friends to come and share a story or a memory. She recounts the day they met—he was selling sketches in the West Village, on the lawn of Saint Vincent's Triangle at 7th Avenue and Greenwich. She bought a drawing for her mother just a week before she passed away. Six months later, they met again at the same park and talked for an hour. That evening, they went out for a drink, and six months after that, they moved in together. They fit like hand in glove and were married within a year.

Katie's oldest friend, Shelby, hooks her arm around Katie's during this story and cries. She has heard it before and was witness to it all. John fit into the friend group, no fractures, no stress. It was a once-in-a-lifetime connection.

After the thank yous, the hugs, and the goodbyes, car doors closed on this chapter of life. Each mourner's life will change, in small and large ways, after this upheaval. The paths they are on have been altered. They may not all realize it yet, but as the cars pull away from Calvary Cemetery in Queens, their lives—and the world—have changed.

* * *

Shelby and Katie have been inseparable for most of their lives. From grade school through their final year of college, they have been joined at the hip. Life, work, and romance have pulled them apart a little, but they remain very close. Even after long hiatuses due to travel or work, conversations are always easy. In recent years, the gaps in communication have grown. But when Shelby heard about John, she raced to the phone.

The second round of dirty martinis arrived a moment ago. The bartender at the White Horse knows exactly how Katie likes them. Extra olive, very easy vermouth, and today, everything is on the house.

"While you were having sex? Are you... I mean, feeling guilty about that?"

"Initially, yeah," says Katie. "But the doctor said it wasn't that. He didn't actually have an explanation. Freak thing, you know?"

"I couldn't imagine." She takes a sip.

"Me neither." Katie shrugs and pokes the pimento out of one of the olives in her drink.

They have a dual sigh, and a sip.

"This is stupid, but I was just thinking about the fish tank story."

Katie nearly spits out her drink laughing.

At a time of tragedy all the emotions ebb and flow. Nature's healing process.

"I felt so bad."

"It was devastation, the poor salamander."

"And the turtle! And the frogs. I can't believe he forgave me."

As the story goes, John brought home a large fish tank he found on the street. Someone had left it out on the curb. A piece of scratch paper taped to the tank had the words "FREE" and "LEAKS" written on it. He had read an article in the "At Home" section of *The New York Times* titled "Make Your Very Own Terrarium" that mentioned using spent fish tanks. The article suggested adding small animals, in addition to the tropical plants, to create a little living Amazon Rainforest. Katie brought home what she thought was a lizard for the jungle eco fish tank. Over time, it grew into a baby alligator. It started eating the frogs and killing the other animals.

This is Katie's first real laugh since John's death.

Memories serve as bridges to healing. Flashes of *what was* to aid the transition to *what is*.

It's a merciful process.

"I thought there would be more time. I mean, being in the apartment is weird. It's 'our' apartment. Thinking about 'our' plans, 'our' dreams, it was all 'our' stuff. Now it's just 'me,'" she shrugs.

"Kate, I know you, and I know you're going to make it, and I'm going to be here. Whatever you need—you're going to be all right."

Retracing

THE CORRUGATED STEEL door of a twenty-foot square storage unit at 161 Varick Street slides open. Cardboard boxes are stacked along the walls. Framed photos and paintings are wrapped in cracking brown paper. Objects of odd shapes rest atop the boxes. The unit is a historical record of John and Katie's past, pre- and post-marriage.

It's full of the things they didn't have room for or couldn't bear to part with. Katie sighs at the sight of an unopened shipping box. It had been sent to her previous address and announced as a "pre-college-graduation" present. Her late parents insisted it was the perfect gift: a wooden sign that reads, "Home is Where the Heart Is." Her mother had suggested she hang it in a place of prominence in her apartment. The box was never opened. It never hung on her wall. It never left the storage unit.

She pulls the heavy canvas off their Jeep, old faithful. It's just as they left it six weeks ago, with the hood cracked open.

Katie disconnects the three-amp Sears trickle charger from the battery and then reconnects the red battery cable with a three-eighths inch open-end wrench that is always left resting on top of the battery. When she opens the driver's door, the dome light clicks on—a good sign. The keys, as usual, are tucked under the driver's side sun visor and drop into her waiting hand. The old truck fires right up.

She crosses the city and drives through Brooklyn. After a while, things start to thin out. City slips to suburbs and again to countryside. A forest of maple and elm trees lines the two lane road.

It's a long drive to Laurel Lake, but Katie knows it well.

Her grandparents raised geese there way back when. The Christmas goose in New York was huge, but the Laurel Lake geese were the best.

The Wagoneer turns off the highway onto Kirkup Lane and then onto a long gravel driveway leading to the old family home. The engine shuts off, its sound replaced by the breeze rustling through the elms and the honking of geese flying south. Ripples, leaves, and a family of ducks float on the calm surface of Laurel Lake.

As is her custom upon arrival, Katie walks to test the waters of the lake. She passes an aluminum rowboat resting upside down on a metal rack near the shore. She knows the oars are hidden beneath, tangled in spider webs from this year and last. Beyond the boat stands an ancient wooden dock, gray from the weather. It has endured rain, sun, and snow. Her grandfather had built it from teak planks he acquired years ago. He was proud of that dock, and it's likely to last forever.

She walks to the end, removes her shoes, and sits. The wood is damp. Her feet dangle in the cold water. Minnows wriggle in the shallows, and a bug scurries across the surface.

So many memories are tied to this place: picnics, swimming, family gatherings. During Katie's childhood, everyone lived nearby and shared in both the good and the bad. This house, and this place, used to be so full of life. The structures still stand, but she's the only one left to enjoy them.

The code for the lockbox on the wall next to the kitchen door is 0-5-2-4. The key with the rubber band wrapped through the hole clinks as Katie opens it. It's the same key for all the doors on the outside of the house, but the kitchen door is the one everyone uses. It's on the prettier side of the house; it faces the lake. The front door and porch face the road and are only used by delivery people and the occasional solicitor. As a little girl, Katie often worried the house might tip over like a ship, since everyone was always in the kitchen.

She lets herself in. Everything is as it should be: the usual dead flies on the windowsill, undoubtedly panicked during their final moments, trapped between the closed window and the not-so-well-fitting screen. A few wispy spiderwebs drape from the light fixture to the cupboards, but no spiders are visible. *Not bad*, she thinks.

Katie makes a quick tour of the first floor. In the living room, sheets drape over the furniture. The lace curtains, cracked from the sun, hang in the window. Empty coat hooks stand next to the front entrance. The house smells a little musty. She opens the front and kitchen doors to take advantage of the usual breeze coming off the lake. That was always the first order of business on arrival—airing out the house.

Down the stairs to the basement, beams of light filter through the ground-level windows. The smell of mothballs lingers, and a few dust specks float in the air. The house feels empty and lonely, clearly unoccupied for a long time.

Up the stairs and along the hallway are generations of photographs. The second door on the left is John and Katie's room. Inside, the bed is stripped, and the dresser and chair stand at attention. The room seems smaller without the pillows, the suitcases, and the sounds of people—the life. Over the dresser, pictures hang: her as a child, as a teen, with her parents, and with John. She blows off the dust.

How did this happen? she wonders. *All the people, all the lives that passed through these rooms.* Her grandparents, who had the misfortune of outliving their own daughter, Katie's mother, by just a year. Aunts, uncles, and friends who visited in the summer. There was always an open door, always a green pear to pick from the tree near the lake, or coffee at the picnic table under that same pear tree. The kids would take out the rowboat to fish with chunks of cheese, jump off the dock into the cool, clear lake, or play marathon games of hide-and-seek among the lilacs and cattails. What an incredible place and time, and how she had taken it for granted.

Those generations seemed indestructible, until they withered and died. The kids became adults, made their own lives, and this all became less important somehow. Katie and John's visits became ever more sparse with the intrusion of upward mobility and career pursuits. "We'll try to get out at Christmas," were the last words she said to her grandparents.

Rhubarb Pie

THE ROADSIDE DINER on State Route 48 has been there as long as Katie can remember, unchanged since her childhood. The stools at the counter look past a belt-driven toaster and chrome coffee machines into the kitchen. Vinyl booths hold menus wedged between ketchup and mustard. A glass case displays the homemade pies and cakes. Same as it ever was.

The staff no longer wears the pale yellow uniforms. That is one of the two signs of the modern age. The other is the $5.95 price tag for a slice of rhubarb pie. Significantly more than when Katie was eight, but the taste is exactly the same. She finds substantial comfort in the sweet, tangy, warm, crusty pie. Nibbling on her second slice and at the bottom of a cup of coffee, she stares outside to the nearby marshlands. A pelican coasts past a heron.

A woman in her mid-sixties sits down at the counter. She is mulling over dessert options with the person taking the order. "Banana cream, apple, or rhubarb pie, what do you think?"

"They're all good," he says.

"Go with the rhubarb," Katie chimes in. "It can't be beat—anywhere."

"That's quite an endorsement. Thank you."

"I have been coming here my whole life, and usually sitting on this same stool. It's a guarantee."

"Rhubarb it is then," the woman says, "and a coffee. Coffee?" she asks Katie. "One good deed deserves another."

"Sure." She holds out her cup to the person behind the counter. "This free refill is on you." They share a chuckle as she adds cream to her coffee. "Join me?"

"*That* is exactly why I'm here today." She slides over one stool. "I'm Brooke."

"Katie."

"Thanks for the invite."

"My grandmother used to bring me here for the rhubarb pie," says Katie. "Simpler times, you know?" Katie takes a pause and looks out the window. "I hope this view never changes—the yellowed glass, the occasional heron."

Brooke follows her gaze. "It certainly is something. Peaceful," says Brooke. The heron takes flight. "I'm glad I decided to stop. This pie is heavenly. Did you come from the city?"

Katie nods, swallowing a sip of the fresh coffee. "On the edge of the West Village— Hudson and 10th."

"My neighborhood, too. I'm sure we know some of the same people. You must know the cupcakes at the Magnolia Bakery?"

"Oh—guilty pleasure," Katie says. "My husband's favorite. He had a sweet tooth—late husband...." Katie's voice cracks at those words. She reaches for a napkin at the involuntary misting of her eyes and the tight closing of her mouth. She chokes out some tears. "Sorry."

"Oh—I'm so sorry."

Katie nods. "Thanks." She dries her eyes.

Knowing when to give someone space is a learned skill. *Have a bite of the pie, compliment the server,* "This really is delicious—could you warm up my coffee a touch?" Some people don't like to talk about sensitive things; some people need to unload.

"It's kind of a fresh wound," Katie says, reigniting the conversation.

She needs to talk, thinks Brooke. "Very unexpected at your age, to say the least."

"Yeah...."

Brooke pushes a short stack of napkins in front of Katie.

Whoever this stranger is, it's great timing. A friendly face to talk to, and someone who will listen.

Katie feels a door open.

She needs a sounding board after her stiff upper lip at the funeral and the ghostly silence at home. Her pilgrimage to the lake house—empty time in empty spaces—is lonely without family or counterpoint. No one to be loud with, no one to be quiet with, just the constant screaming of her own mind, running over regrets. Things they had not done. Things she had presumed would eventually happen, despite perpetual postponements.

She tells Brooke about John's death, omitting the intimate details. She talks about the company she poured her heart into for more than a decade and shares emotions and regrets she wouldn't even express to her therapist.

"Let me ask you something, Katie, and forgive me if this sounds corny. Have you ever looked at the night sky and wondered if there's life out there? Or why a flock of birds all turn together? Or how things always seem to work out at the very last moment? Or how something that seems like nonsense now becomes obvious later?"

"Yes, but...."

"What does that have to do with anything?" Brooke continues Katie's thought. "John dying was part of the plan, Katie. Death is part of life, and everyone leaves their mark on the world. John did, and so did his passing."

Katie thinks of a picture of John and her from New Year's Eve three years ago.

"I'm just suggesting that we don't know everything and that there's magic in the world. I believe that if we take our knowledge and best ideas, we can use them to make small adjustments in the world. Those will ripple into massive changes for humanity—pretty lucky if you ask me. We can each have the greatest job in the Universe."

"Do you think that's true?"

"I'm certain of it."

Letting all this out, and hearing Brooke's fresh perspective, makes something clear. This is an opportunity to reset. To decide and establish what the rest of her life will be. She will return to the city, take stock, and start again.

"You probably aren't ready to get back to work yet, but we're looking for someone. I think you could not be more perfect for it."

Katie pushes some crust around on her plate. Her lips form a grateful smile.

"We are influencers of a sort. It's philanthropy, travel—we have a worldwide reach. A bunch of globally-connected, forward thinking do-gooders who make a difference in almost everyone's life on the planet. Do you want to come by the office and chat?"

In that moment, Katie thinks, *I am blessed*. She can't commit to anything, or even have a serious discussion. It is too soon. Her life has been turned upside down, and that's not a good place to start from. But to be wanted—to be recognized as "perfect" for something—it feels good. She wonders if her inner smile is showing through. "I'm not ready yet," she says. "But thank you. Really."

"I believe things happen for a reason, Katie. The Universe has a plan."

Brooke pulls out an old business card and flips it over to write on the back. "I'm going to give you my number. If you change your mind, or just want to talk, or meet me for a slice of pie—anytime." Brooke hands Katie the card; "Paul & Sons Bookseller," it says on one side, with Brooke's name and number on the other.

"'Paul & Sons...,' my last name is Paulson, funny."

"It's a great little shop, one of my favorites. They have the most delightful art on the walls." Brooke stands to leave. "I need to get on the road, but I'll see you soon—I'm sure of it."

Katie surprises herself by standing up and giving her a hug. "Thank you."

"You're going to be all right," says Brooke.

That is just what Shelby had said. *The Universe is being encouraging*, Katie thinks.

On the long ride back to the city, Katie puts on "Revolution Number One" (the lesser-known version of the classic) from The Beatles' self-titled *White Album*. She sings along and knows it's going to be all right. She puts the sun visor down on the passenger side to block the afternoon glare.

The postcard John had doodled on flutters down from the visor and lands in her lap. The two of them in the same boat.

She lets the tears come, willing herself into the future the Universe has given her.

New Reality

Days, weeks.

Trees drop their colorful leaves and the winds carry them away.

Katie examines the landscape of John's desk, which sits next to the radiator. He always liked the warmth, and the view, from that spot. She bounces gently on his exercise ball chair—something she had been threatening to throw out for years. She needs to go through the mail: there's an unpaid bill, a form "thank you" letter for a Red Cross donation they had made in lieu of giving blood, a stack of credit card and loan offers, and a *Westways* magazine from the Auto Club. On the cover, a good-looking couple is having the best time in a gorgeous tropical destination.

They planned to find a vacation spot this year for sure. They were overdue.

Last year as a birthday present, John had booked what promised to be a fun and saucy sojourn. A tour of distilleries in Scotland. But some Madison Avenue clients insisted they needed Katie's help on the "look" for an ad campaign. The color scheme wasn't quite right, they said—six times. The trip got postponed.

The year before, they had tickets to fly to Buenos Aires, then take a week to drive to Tierra del Fuego. See the sights, see the penguins. But there were two important holiday parties—it was December. These parties were a necessary evil for staying in the minds of important clients. They decided to postpone South America.

The weight of accepting the hustle of mid-life suddenly hit Katie. What had she been thinking? How important is any of it now? There won't be a trip to Reykjavík, or Thanksgiving in Montauk, or chiding each other about having a kid.

She remembers her parents' deaths. The consensus from friends and her own research is clear: don't make any big decisions for at least a year. Selling houses, stocks, or cars—there's no rush, and she has found many accounts of people regretting their snap decisions. *Makes sense*, she thinks.

The little things are more confusing, though—like clothes. John's clothes still hang in their closet and the front hall. He loved his "jackets for every occasion" collection: three sport coats—blue, camel hair, and cream; two rain jackets, one insulated; a leather motorcycle jacket (which began as a Halloween costume); a vintage jean jacket; and two down jackets, one light and one heavy.

Food. She's not someone who likes sweet pickles, Miracle Whip, or those "healthy" crackers that taste like sawdust.

Reading materials. John regularly bought books and magazines—travel and outdoor publications, books on living off the grid, and periodicals on gardening and identifying wild mushrooms. Katie sometimes referred to him in conversation as "my little forager."

All these things made up John's world, none more than his stupid exercise ball chair.

But now, all of it is precious. All of it is *him*.

Katie hasn't mourned like this before. It is vastly different than when her parents passed. The worst part, she found, is not having the day-to-day. Not having someone to talk to, to wake up with. Not having someone to get mad at or quietly admire. The pain subsides a little every day, but the emptiness, along with the ball chair, remains.

Lucie DuBois

1783
Eastern Europe

THE UNIVERSE SENDS them to Prague, the capital of Bohemia. For just over a year, they lay the groundwork for the Emperor Francis Chain Bridge. Decades later, that bridge will be the site of an accident involving a carriage, a wagon, and two wild dogs. The eventual grandmother of a future serial killer will be badly injured, redirecting her family's lineage.

Next, they move to Lausanne, in the canton of Vaud, Switzerland, for another eight or nine months. Their tasks ensure that Lord Byron (the poet) and Mary Shelley will meet. Their meeting inspires her novel *Frankenstein*, which has thrilled millions since its publication.

Then they move on to Geneva, still an independent city-state, not yet part of an official Switzerland. The reason for this move is to carry out a single, simple task—a task that seems unimportant.

Geneva, thinks the woman, *must be one of the most*

beautiful places in the world. The immense lake, fed by the melting snow from the surrounding peaks, is home to geese, swans, and ducks swimming in its clear, cold waters. The charm of its grand architecture and vibrant culture excites the senses. Even in summer, snow caps the peaks of the Swiss Alps, cutting into the deep blue sky.

To lie in the sun, feel the breeze off the lake, and listen to the wildlife—"*Heaven,*" the woman says to herself. She and the boy fall asleep there one afternoon, the day especially perfect. A nap by the lakeside, followed by a walk through the city, admiring the structures and inhaling the aromas of pastries from the boulangeries.

The next morning, in their small, one-room apartment, the boy begs for another day just like that one, the blue sky, the light breeze. He wants to toss more scraps of stale bread to the waterfowl that gather at the lakeside and dip his toes in the water. It can't hurt to take a day off. She sees the look in his eyes, the joy of this child—her child.

He has been dragged across continents, asked to sacrifice again and again. Yet, his life is undoubtedly better than it would have been if she hadn't saved him that night in Rome so long ago. The way the light comes through the window and lights up his face—his dark curls and pleading smile—the woman finds herself lost in his charm and sweetness. Saying no is impossible. When she tells him, "Yes, of course we can," and he runs to her, she is met with joy, glee, and the deep, clutching embrace of a grateful child. It is love. And what is better than that?

They will take the day, be together, and have fun. Such a rarity, to have fun. They will find another task to do tomorrow. Today's seems almost entirely meaningless and routine.

She and the boy are meant to go to the Maison de Poste,

one of several facilities for beginning stagecoach travel from Geneva. They are to book a journey to Marseille on a particular day at a particular time. The journey usually takes several days, and weather can sometimes slow things down. There will be stops to refresh or change the horses and to sleep and eat at roadside inns near Lyon, or Avignon.

"Space on the coach is limited," the instructions say. *"Pack only one change of clothes. Bring dried meat, dried fruit, nuts, and water enough for three people. There will be a young woman traveling alone, Lucie DuBois. She will not have food or money to stay at the inns. She will be sleeping outside and inconspicuously collecting food during stops. Offer food and shelter,"* the instructions continue, *"and kind conversation."*

"Someone will certainly help this Lucie DuBois," the woman says to the boy.

One simple gesture of kindness.

With help, Lucie DuBois will make it to Marseille and board a boat to Barcelona. (The combination of land and sea is the least painful way to make the journey at this point in time.) Upon arrival in Barcelona, she will be met by her cousin at the docks. In the next week, she will be introduced to someone who needs French-speaking help in a kitchen. She speaks French and Spanish fluently; this opportunity must be seized.

At home, she has been the right hand to her mother and grandmother in the kitchen since she could stand.

Her mother is a wonderful cook, but her grandmother is the real genius. They are always vying for the praise of their family, their friendly culinary competition always amusing Lucie.

One year, not so long ago, in early April—the prime time for salmon spawning—the men came home from the

Allier River with two beautiful, pregnant, roe-filled salmon. Their shiny silver and black skin glistened, and their flesh was dark and rich.

A meal was prepared, to be shared with the entire clan on a beautiful late spring evening in the Loire Valley. The two women doing the cooking had the same ingredients, worked in the same kitchen, and prepared the same main dish. (The kids and menfolk helped with the salads, sides, and desserts.) At mealtime, fifteen people sat at a long wooden table among the cherry trees heavy with ripe, sweet fruit. Two main dishes of saumon à l'orange were laid out side by side. The grandmother had the clear advantage.

Everyone agreed there must be some kind of magic following her.

It has been surmised that some of this magic passed to her granddaughter, who, with help from the Universe, could have arrived in Barcelona at the right time.

One night at the restaurant, the young woman will be preparing a meal for herself with the leftovers from the evening. There will be, she finds, the ingredients for her grandmother's saumon à l'orange. So, she will start the sauce, prepare the fish, and sit down, tired from the day but thinking of home, to enjoy it.

The scent of the dish will captivate the cook who hired her. He will insist on a taste. Then insist on the recipe. Months later, the cook will propose marriage, and a short time after that, become locally renowned for salmón en salsa de naranja.

All this thanks to Lucie DuBois who spent time with her grandmother perfecting the French version of the dish. The chef will be ordered to cook for King Ferdinand VII of Spain.

The chef's half-brother is part of a rebel group against

the King. He supports the recently renounced liberal constitution of Spain. (The constitution was abolished by King
Ferdinand when he retook the throne in 1814.) The brother
will visit the palace and, unbeknownst to the chef, poison a
meal. The King and his entire family will be killed. The
First Carlist War (1833–1839), a fight over control of Spain
after Ferdinand's passing, will be entirely avoided. And
because there will be no First Carlist War, there will be no
Second or Third Carlist War. Many thousands of lives will
be spared and the face of Europe changed forever.

But no one helps Lucie DuBois.

She is arrested in Avignon for stealing food. "J'ai très
faim!" she says over and over to the innkeeper, who beats
her and calls his cousin, the local gendarme. Lucie never
makes the boat to Barcelona, never meets the cook, never
gets married or shares a recipe which thrills a king.

She dies of cholera in a subterranean cell in the south of
France.

The woman and the boy do not know these things. Not
yet. Then there is a knock on their door.

Bonjour, Guten Morgen, Good Morning

1801

Paris

THE BOY IS ASLEEP. Someone knocks again at the door. "Attendez, s'il vous plaît," the woman says as she quietly cracks open the door. A slender man with salt and pepper hair who looks in his forties, and a round-faced woman a bit younger, stand before her. "Oui?"

"Bonjour," says the man.

"Guten Morgen," says the round-faced woman, extending her hand and offering a calling card—black with a blue circle in the center. "Welche Sprache sprechen Sie am liebsten?"

"Oh, hallo. Englisch, bitte? Ich habe es gelernt."

"Very good! Learning English. This will be to your advantage. I am Rae," she says, "and this is Leo." She again offers the calling card.

This is what she has seen since the beginning. On every message she has received, including the first. The calling card, the blue circle on the black.

"How is the boy? May we come in?"

They know about the boy? The woman eases back in the doorway, studying their faces and voices carefully. Though she has lived in many places across Germany and France, these people don't seem familiar.

She and the boy have moved every year, never staying in one place long enough to get to know anyone too well. After all, getting too close to people is part of the problem. The boy is barely aging, and she herself seems to also stay the same.

Disappearing is easier than being accused of sorcery, or worse. She has followed the instructions marked with the same black and blue symbols—do this task, travel to this city.

Most of the instructions, anyway.

She thinks of the window in Peder Rasmussen's tailor shop in Copenhagen, which she failed to break. A young Dane with auburn hair and stunning green eyes had invited her for a walk. "Of course," she said, and she left the boy with a neighbor. This young, handsome man is long dead, as are his children. A candle burned too long in Peder Rasmussen's shop, and a bit of fabric hanging too close to it caught fire. The candle would have been blown out if the window had been broken. The resulting 1728 fire destroyed much of the city.

She remembers befriending Sophia, the daughter of a Swedish nobleman, during a stay in Stockholm. They were digging up tulip bulbs from the thawing earth in the late eighteenth century. The day was too perfect and the weather too welcome to do anything else. She forgot to cut loose the horses from his carriage that day. The same evening, the nobleman shot King Gustav III of Sweden during a masked ball at the Royal Opera House. The king took almost three weeks to die, and the country was forever changed.

"May we come in?" asks Rae again.

"We are here to discuss your debt," says Leo.

The woman recalls the words on the invitation:

"The debt repaid awaits another life. Embrace the Universe; the world shall change."

She can feel her heartbeat accelerating, her palms clutched and sweaty. "I do not know you. Excuse me." She begins to close the door.

"The boy is in danger—you both are. Please, may we come in?"

"Please."

* * *

The three of them sit around a small, round wooden table. The woman has only two chairs, one of which needs repair. Leo sits on a wooden crate turned on its side which normally holds the small split logs burned for heat in the winter. *"Château Margaux"* is burned into the side of it.

A prized souvenir rests in the center of the table: a Moroccan tea set. Curved silver patterns are gracefully etched into it, even on its arching handle. The small glass cups in their decorative silver sleeves hold warm, sweet, amber green mint tea.

The eight months spent in Morocco were full of discovery—foods, spices, camels, monkeys. The Berber people with their shocking eyes, the Arabs, the Andalusian Jews, and the Sub-Saharan Africans. Olive skin covered with beautiful fabrics and jewels. She would have stayed in the country if not for the task to ship out to Constantinople. *When will the debt be repaid?*

She discovers that her history was unknown to Rae and Leo, except for her tasks from the Universe. Of those, they seemed to know all the details—the times, places, accuracy of what was done, and the repercussions.

The woman gasps at the recounting of some of their stories. And the consequences when the tasks are done wrong, or not at all.

She comes to realize that they are more *orders* than tasks. She is learning about aspects of her agreement with the Universe.

They recount the story of Thomasine Osborne. "What can be done?" she asks. "Can it be corrected?"

The woman remembers; it was so long ago. Another lifetime it seems. *You will enjoy a long and fruitful life.*

They speak in metaphor: "It's a winding river with many distributaries; things always flow, and unexpected things happen." They insist she not feel alone, saying, "There are others like us in the world. There have been other mistakes. We help each other."

She weeps at the death of Lucie DuBois and the coming wars because of her failure. Again, "What can be done?" she pleads. "Can it be corrected?"

"It may take hundreds of years and be left to your successor—the one you will find, teach, and guide into taking on the tasks as you were guided." *The debt repaid awaits another life.*

"What will happen with the boy?" she asks.

They don't know; it doesn't work that way. The imperfection in the process creates variables that are unpredictable. The exact moment of executing an order may or may not be ideal.

Adjustments will have to be made in the future to keep things flowing in the right direction. "That's what we hope for," says Leo. "Adjustments too far off bring unforeseen problems." *Look to the future, where souls may be saved....*

A chill flashes through the woman.

They tell a story of a possible road back to where things should be if the woman and the boy had not strayed off course. It isn't too late to change the future, to prevent certain family tragedies, halt untimely deaths, and avoid unnecessary births. To make sacrifices for the greater good.

"There will be sacrifice and difficult decisions ahead," says Rae.

"Of course."

"You must not veer from the tasks. Do you understand?" asks Leo.

"Yes."

"Lives depend on it, including yours."

"You may be killed."

"How?" the woman desperately asks. "Can I somehow prepare? Look ahead, past the immediate tasks?"

Rae explains it is only a matter of asking. "Remove the black-inked square and the blue circle from an order and burn it. The next order in the sequence of events will be delivered."

The woman found she could look even further ahead by burning the orders as they arrived instead of waiting for them to be executed. She went back through the bound stack of the hundreds of orders to tear corners and then burn them.

Her vision begins to extend deeper into the future— things she can't understand, people she can't imagine, in places she has never heard of. *What is tour bus?* she thinks. *Where is Quebec?*

She is ready to follow the instructions and assemble the

pieces. This is a puzzle, she decides; some pieces must be made to fit.

She has the power to save the boy.

Slowly, the tasks continue, and the travel continues. She believes the Universe keeps them moving to hide this eternal boy, who continues to grow so, so slowly. She too has barely aged, still with the face of a young woman.

Hungry for clues and knowledge, she reads everything she can find. She looks for things that align with future orders and past problems. She reads stories about the new American colonies of England, the war in the New World, and Napoleon losing his mind across Europe.

When the Netherlands defeat Napoleon, an order arrives: take the boy to Rotterdam.

Paul & Sons

ALMOST EVERY DAY, there are some pieces of her previous life to pick up. The laundry ticket under the magnet on the refrigerator door is one. John had dropped off a couple of shirts at the dry cleaner. Now is as good a time as any to fetch them.

Katie has gotten in the habit of taking alternate routes through the neighborhood, avoiding the places she and John frequented. Fewer reminders of their everyday life. Discovering new places and things that have popped up keeps her mood buoyant. Shops regularly appear and sometimes disappear just as quickly. Last week, a new art gallery, a healthy juice shop, and two high-end clothing boutiques opened their doors. A hardware store shuttered after fifty-eight years. The slow evolution of small-town New York trudges forward. Many of the older mom-and-pop shops—cobblers, tailors, locksmiths—have been priced out. No one really gets shoes fixed or has suits custom-made anymore. Culture is more disposable, fashion more fleeting, and door-knobs now have electronic codes.

Katie's father had a locksmith business in the neighborhood. Inside the tiny, ten-by-ten-foot sliver of a shop, thousands of keys hung on hooks. Fobs and rings of all colors were neatly presented in transparent display boxes, and a modest selection of padlocks sat in a small glass case under the cash register. He never sold combination locks in hopes that buyers would come back for a key when they lost one.

When he died, a neighbor took over the business. About six months later, they gave it up. "Too slow, can't pay the rent," they had said. Katie imagines her dad's love of chatting and cribbage is what had kept him in business. Most days, weather permitting, there was a card table set up on the sidewalk out front. People who needed keys would wait for a pause in the action, or sometimes sit in and play a hand while her dad made the keys. Katie had learned to play pinochle at that table, but that was a lifetime ago.

In recent years, the space has been a single-chair hair weaver, a cigarette shop, and is now a miniature tattoo shop. "Pete's Tats," it's called. And they're having a special today. *"Twenty-five percent off your first tattoo,"* reads the sign outside the shop.

Katie hasn't been down this block in years, but it feels nice to think of her dad today. She peeks into the tattoo shop. There's a college girl in an orange t-shirt getting "I Love NY" tattooed onto her calf.

Half a block down the street is a sandwich board sign painted white, with a black chalkboard on the bottom two-thirds. *"BUY ONE GET ONE FREE (of same or lesser value)"* reads the handwritten note on the sign. The O's have smiley faces drawn inside of them. At the top of the sign is the name of the shop: "Paul & Sons Booksellers, est. 1939."

Brooke, the woman she advised on the rhubarb pie, had scrawled her phone number on the back of a card from this same shop. *What are the odds?* Katie thinks. She has been on this block countless times and has never even noticed it.

Katie makes a mental note to return and have a look inside. A moment later, a crack of thunder and a few chunks of sleet direct her down the few steps into the basement bookshop.

Katie pushes open the glass door tucked under the staircase. An old-fashioned brass bell rings. A man in his late sixties, Katie guesses, is behind the small checkout counter. He leans against a stool thumbing through a *Cook's Illustrated* magazine. "Afternoon," he says. She smiles and drifts into the shop. She can hear the hail falling outside.

Uneven shelves, floor to ceiling, fill in every bit of space. The shelves look as though they have been collected at rummage sales over the years. The vent of an air conditioner is barely visible through stacks of unsorted hardcovers and paperbacks on a shelf below it.

"Genres are on the red cards," the proprietor says, pointing to a shelf. "They're alphabetical by author—mostly."

"Thank you."

This is the kind of place a person could spend a week in and still have only seen a fraction of it. *Seeing so many books I've never heard of with important-sounding titles is intimidating*, thinks Katie.

Hemingway and Vonnegut, Tolkien, Fitzgerald, Woolf, Morrison and Shelley. She walks by a torn, yellowed copy of *Slaughterhouse-Five*; there's one in the lake house. She remembers reading it as a teenager. Same with Orwell's *1984*.

Dickinson, Whitman, Frost, Wilde, Browning, Keats, Wordsworth. Her grandfather would sit under the pear tree in a wicker chair with any one of those poets for hours.

There's a painting on the wall, explosive yellow flowers. The artist's name is obscured by a short stack of Dr. Seuss books. It's abstract, vivid, joyous. It reminds her of a week-long trip they took to Ontario, Canada—she stood in a field surrounded by thousands of sunflowers in bloom. John wanted to draw ducks. *There's a photo of that somewhere,* she imagines.

Sleet collects in a window high on the wall toward the back of the space. She walks through the light and at the end of the overflowing shelving, there is an open area. A desk, maybe for book signings. A leather chair, maybe for storytime, and more artwork on the walls.

In the serene little spot, a teenage girl browses a volume on Egyptian culture. An old woman adjusts her glasses and checks the price on the inside cover of a well-used French cookbook.

A drawing on the wall catches Katie's eye. Then another. She is looking at an intentional display, maybe an exhibit. A bird's nest, in pen and ink. The nest is empty, the branches are bare, and a little snow is collected on one of them. In the next drawing, the same nest. Buds are starting to form, and a couple of leaves are growing. A bird stands on the edge of the nest, holding a string in its beak. It's building its home, like the bird outside the window next to John's desk. In the next drawing, the bird sits atop three eggs. Its partner has just taken flight, halfway out of the frame. Leaves fill the branches. In the next drawing, both birds feed their young. Their eager, gaping mouths want to consume anything their parents can supply. Two more drawings: one bird alone in the nest. No babies, no partner. The leaves on the branches are sparse. In the last drawing, much like the first, bare branches, raindrops, an empty nest. A tear rolls down

Katie's cheek. She has seen this before, right outside her own window year after year.

She steps in for a closer look to see who the artist is.

The drawings are stunning. The lines seem so familiar, the highlight in the eye of the mother, the detail in the feathers.

Gracefully signed with black ink in the lower right corner are two words she has seen countless times: *"John Paulson."*

Meet Again

"Hello?"

The voice on the other end of the call is warm and calm.

"Brooke?"

"Yes."

"It's Katie—I don't know if you remember me, but we met over some rhubarb pie."

"Katie! Of course!" Brooke's voice brings her right back to their first meeting. "I knew you'd call."

"I'm sorry it's been a minute. I needed some time." *Of course she did.*

"We've all been through it, Katie. Some more than others. You did the right thing. Use your time for what *you* need. It's all part of the grand plan. Right now, you're exactly where you should be."

"I was out yesterday," Katie says, "and I don't know if you remember, but you wrote your number on the back of a business card from a bookshop."

"'Paul & Sons,' I remember. I love that shop."

"I stumbled across it. It's a real gem. This is going to

sound like the world's biggest coincidence, but in the back...."

"The reading area?"

"Yes, in the reading area, they have a series of sketches on the wall."

"Oh! The bird's nest! Believe it or not, I actually bought those from a street artist years ago and donated them to the shop. Not donated exactly, but in exchange for a couple of old collectible volumes I had been hunting for. I'm probably the only person in the city who wanted them."

"You bought them? When?"

"It had to be twenty years ago. They were just irresistible."

Twenty years ago. That was before Katie and John met. Katie's parents were in the bus accident nineteen years ago, which led to them getting pneumonia and being admitted to the downtown hospital. Katie had bought one of John's drawings for her mother while she was in the hospital.

"I'm not superstitious, but this sure looks like a sign from somewhere. The artist, Brooke—you're not going to believe this—was my husband. My late husband. Twenty years ago was before we had even met!"

Katie hears a gasp on the other end of the line, followed by a laugh. "That is unbelievable, Katie. I mean, what are the chances, in a city of millions?! What do you think it all means?"

"An omen, a sign. When we ran into each other the last time, you said you knew we'd meet again."

"I hoped."

"I would never have imagined that John would be involved in us meeting. He would be entertained by this for sure."

"What do you think he'd say?"

Katie immediately knows the answer to that question, and the knowing makes her quietly smile. She sees him, sketching in the park, sleeping on the couch, or proposing a stop for any kind of dessert. He wanted her to live her life, get away from the rat race, and do something that brought her joy. He wanted her to stop worrying about reaching the top of anything and to get down to the core of the funny, kind, and caring person he knew she was.

"I think he'd say I should see it as a door opening, and I should go through to see what's on the other side. I'll either find something amazing or discover another door."

Even though Brooke and Katie couldn't see each other's faces, they knew by the silence that they should meet again.

"I think we should get a piece of pie, Katie. What do you think?"

"I think so too. And I'm ready to start the next chapter, Brooke. Can we talk about this job that I'm so perfect for?"

"How about you stop by the office, and I'll make a fresh pot of coffee? There's a non-disclosure agreement to sign, and then I can show you around and we can discuss work and schedule some pie."

"Tomorrow okay for you?"

"Perfect."

Katie writes down the address—Queens.

Welcome to Queens

HOLIDAY DECORATIONS LITTER THE CITY, and the morning winter sun lights up dingy patches of dirty snow. Katie walks four blocks from the nearby 39th Avenue subway station in Queens, scanning addresses on buildings as she moves at her usual Manhattan pace.

Sweet-smelling smoke rises from a cart selling roasted nuts. It's planted in front of the building she's headed for— an unremarkable block and concrete box of a building near 34th Street and 38th Avenue. This is the address Brooke gave her.

At the nut vendor, a kid screeches for a bag of the sweet treat. The mom loses the battle, exchanging a five dollar bill for temporary silence.

"That would not be my kid," Katie mumbles, as any delusional, anticipatory parent might say.

She pushes through the glass door into a stark lobby. To the left, a closed title insurance business; to the right, an elevator. *"Third floor,"* Brooke had said.

Three white walls in the twelve-by-twenty-foot waiting room surround six chairs, two plants, and a glass table. A stack of *National Geographic* magazines sits neatly centered on the table. The fourth wall is made of frosted glass. It hides whatever office activity is going on behind it. Katie sees two fuzzy figures milling behind the glass. Someone is playing the radio.

"It could use a few photographs or something," she remarks. Katie looks at her watch, on time as always. She unlocks her phone. No coverage. No messages.

Sitting seems impossible. Her body, full of nervous energy, has to move. She takes a lap around the waiting room and glances at the *National Geographic* on the top of the stack. An Olympic swimmer in mid-dive is on the cover.

"You made it!" a voice from behind Katie says. It's Brooke, in business casual and eyeglasses. She carries a clipboard.

Brooke extends her hand, and Katie gives her a hug.

"I can't believe the bookshop," says Brooke.

"Must be destiny," Katie jokes.

"Welcome to the most exciting and least glamorous office in New York. We keep it humble around here, but the perks are great." Katie smiles. "The boss makes me do this— can you have a look at this NDA? It's mostly boilerplate."

"Of course, I understand."

"I took the liberty of filling in your name and the date."

Pretty standard stuff, Katie thinks. *Definition, obligations, exclusions, term.* "A fifty year term?"

"That seemed strange to me, too."

Katie raises her right hand. "I will not discuss any details during this lifetime."

Brooke laughs; Katie signs.

The reunion is exactly as Katie anticipated. Shocking how a stranger can feel so remarkably familiar.

Brooke walks Katie into an office bullpen, an open area

with a few empty freestanding cubicles. A couple dozen frosted glass doors line the perimeter, each with a number stenciled on it. A crooked sign hangs from a chain across an elevator door; it reads, "Out of Service."

Brooke explains again, "We are essentially 'influencers.'" Katie wonders how someone so sweet could be associated with such an annoying profession—something so pervasive in the modern age. "It's all very behind-the-scenes," Brooke continues. "If no one notices you're doing your job, you're doing it right."

That part is appealing. Katie doesn't like the spotlight. She enjoys a sense of accomplishment, rewards based on merit, and being part of a process for the greater good.

"Today, for example, Katie," Brooke says, extracting a sheet from a stack of papers and adjusting her glasses, "we will be helping with a water pipeline that will soon be under construction in North Africa." She holds up the page. It's an outline of sorts, with bullet points and timestamps. Katie can't get a close look, but it seems to be a plan. "We're pulling some strings to open the necessary doors." Brooke pulls out another sheet. "In Springfield, Illinois, we are fixing a traffic signal. It will prevent a multi-vehicle collision with serious consequences."

Katie doesn't want to correct Brooke's tense; she is talking about the future. She knows older people sometimes get confused, and there is no need to emphasize the negative. She likes what Brooke talking about—the greater good, opportunities for living well, for truly living.

Simply stated, that is exactly what Katie wants: to live, to feel alive. She's missed too many shining moments in her life. John would say the same. He was the one planning for the future, setting dates, figuring out itineraries, and finding the best spots for their activities. And she was the preoccupied observer, the attendee. Look how that turned out.

Inside Brooke's office, the two women sit across from each other at her desk. The office has a museum-like quality, but not the quiet, simple, and stately feel of public areas. It's more like the back rooms where artwork is restored or documents archived. Stacks of loose papers, books, and spiral notebooks cover her desk and shelves. Strings connect drawings, pictures, and documents on a cork-covered wall—it's chaotic. Every surface is loaded, and the wall resembles either a treasure map or a crime scene. *Some color-coding might be nice*, Katie thinks.

"Do you mind if we talk about the benefits again? There are a couple of parts that I don't quite understand," Katie says.

"Of course. The basic overview is that we offer full medical, dental, and vision care. We will subsidize your housing and have groceries delivered bi-weekly," Brooke explains. "We also provide a transportation stipend and a phone if you need one. And when we officially sign the contract, time will slow down for you."

Time will slow down. Katie is smiling on the inside. She crosses her feet under the chair, clenching her body to restrain the gleeful laugh bubbling beneath the surface. This is a job interview and a business meeting. She listens intently, encouraging Brooke to continue talking, afraid that if she says anything, it will be accompanied by a suppressed laugh.

The explanation of benefits seems normal and then absurd. *What the hell*, she thinks, *does it really matter?* This adorable older woman brought Katie back from the edge; so what if she's a little "out there?" Katie likes it—she likes *her*.

New York is full of colorful characters, but none that feel like your favorite great aunt.

* * *

"Welcome aboard, Katie," Brooke says with a handshake. "I want to show you a little bit more about what we do here, how we make a difference. When I say 'influencers,' this is what I mean. Remember—it's all behind-the-scenes. Let's watch."

Brooke picks up a remote control and starts a video.

On the old Quasar TV, a young woman dressed in loose clothing is sitting cross-legged and talking to an unseen person.

"I feel so blessed. I want to go and hug the first person I see, with consent of course. The Universe has brought me so much joy. Some people poo-poo that idea, but I know in my heart of hearts that it's true. I would never have reached this pinnacle of happiness without all those little hints from out there." She raises her arms to the sky. "I'm so lucky." The frame freezes.

"You see that joy?" Brooke asks Katie. "Gratitude plays a big role in everyone's life." Katie wonders if she expressed enough gratitude toward John.

Another video starts. It's a middle-aged man in a hospital bed. "This is the worst day of my life. But you know what? I'm okay with it. We had a good run, and nothing is forever. The Universe works in mysterious ways. It brought us together, and now... like I said, a good run."

"Acceptance," Brooke says. "By sharing this with his loved ones, he offers them strength and peace for when he's gone. It's a gift they might not have had otherwise."

A bit of static, then an unkempt, sour-looking man of

retirement age appears on the screen. "I have potential, you know, but I'm stuck being a delivery boy," he says, spitting out his words. "My partner left me for their dog-walker, and my so-called 'friends' won't talk to me. They say I'm bitter— assholes. Somebody has to suffer so others can be happy. That's just the way of the world. If I ever meet the Universe, I'll punch them in the teeth."

"Bitterness," Brooke says. "He needed to hit a low point. Then, he had to shift from blaming others to owning his life. If we don't own our lives Katie—what then?" Brooke raises her eyebrows and gives Katie a reassuring smile.

The scene now shifts to what looks like the inside of the office where Katie and Brooke are sitting. An exotic-looking man in his mid-forties steps into frame. His caramel skin and green eyes contrast with his ill-fitting white short-sleeve shirt and clip-on tie. He looks uncomfortable.

"Hi, my name is Mike Romano. I work in this nondescript office building in Queens, New York." He gestures stiffly around the room. "And these testimonials are all one hundred percent correct."

Katie wonders if the whole thing is some sort of infomercial or snake oil sales pitch.

"I know this for one simple reason. I am one of the employees at the Universe. We are a small operation based in New York, but we're globally connected. My coworkers and I influence everyone around the world every day, with almost everything they do. Throughout the day, we receive stacks of ideas, desires, and information. We passively transmit this information to consumers, right into their brains."

Mike steps closer to the camera for dramatic effect.

"This is a little-known fact, but no one, not a single individual, has an important, original idea." He smiles, feigning confidence.

A black and blue logo flies onto the screen as the video ends.

"You're wondering if it's real," Brooke says as she comes around the desk.

Katie's half-smile and nod agree.

"You're going to see some things that will blow your mind, Katie. You were handpicked for this job. I knew it when we met. I have been looking for you for decades."

Katie has to smile at the exaggeration.

"Dare I say, 'you're the one'—you could really change the world. You just have to believe."

Katie sees nothing but truth in Brooke's kind eyes.

"I took the liberty of making this for you, Katie." Brooke pulls a thick, handmade book from a shelf. "This is everything that brought us together. Everything which was nudged, influenced, and adjusted over my time here at the Universe."

It resembles an encyclopedic scrapbook, tattered and hand-bound.

"It can be confusing how things connect, but it's all there—the clues, the hints, the secrets—everything that explains how you and I ended up together, in this room, today. I thought you'd like to know, Katie."

This feels like an extreme version of the "everything happens for a reason" cliché. Katie has said it herself many times, mostly repeating John.

She flips through the pages filled with tiny text—photocopies of sketches, articles, diagrams, and notes.

"Like destiny?" Katie asks.

"A roadmap for destiny, yes," Brooke replies. "We have

ways to examine more detail than what can fit on a piece of paper, but this will be helpful for reference."

Katie flips through a few pages and lands on one filled with handwritten Spanish text. "I'll take a look," she says, knowing it's something to save for a rainy day—or maybe a week or month down the line.

"Understanding takes time," Brooke says with a hint of pride. "But I have a little personal brag—I've become quite good at connecting the dots and shaping things. Seeing beyond just the 'work orders' from the Universe. You will too."

"Freelancing?"

"In a way," Brooke nods, "but mostly using my accumulated knowledge to see the *intention* behind the work. Sometimes that's less obvious. Enlightenment comes with age and experience. We put the puzzle pieces of our past together to shape our future."

Katie wonders what *her* puzzle pieces are—the fractured parts of her family, the unfulfilled promises, the choices she'd change if she could go back. But she knows she can't. Her only options lie ahead, and that's where her focus has to stay.

"I feel like every day, I have more to learn," Katie says.

"I can't wait for you to get started," Brooke replies. "Your first day here will leave you breathless."

The elevator seems bigger, brighter, cleaner on the way down. Katie is beaming. She needs something to believe in. It's been a rough stretch. "*Bing,*" she mimics the chime of the elevator as she descends.

The elevator doors open and a man with a familiar face

is waiting to get in. It takes her a moment to realize that it's Mike from the video she was just watching. He looks a little older, less chipper.

Back on the street, it's noisy. Big trucks pass by, and the same kid is still there, screaming for nuts. *Asking for another bag*, Katie wonders?

She walks toward the 39th Avenue subway station, her phone to her ear. "Shelby—hi, yes—I'm good, great actually. I'm in Queens. I took a job—yes! I think the whole thing might be a scam, but I love these people, and honestly, what the hell else am I doing?" She listens.

"No, no—not stealing or anything unethical. Just take a pinch of secret society, sprinkle in a bit of Lutheranism, and add a teaspoon of Carl Sagan."

Cemetery

EVEN IN THE dead of winter, the Calvary Cemetery looks breathtaking. The bare trees, gentle slopes, centuries of grave markers and New York City pulsing in the background. Katie walks a now-familiar path to spend a little time with John.

"Shelby says hi," she says as she swaps out the old, dead flowers on the grave for a new bouquet. This one with greens, reds, and golds—Christmas flair. "These are more festive."

She flicks a few leaves away from his grave. "I have some news—I took a position at what I believe is a non-profit. Yes, I said non-profit," she adds with a wry smile. "I know, right? I think doing a little good right now will do *me* some good, and I also thought you'd find that funny."

John was her best friend. She misses the times when they did absolutely nothing together. He was so good at that —easygoing, somehow always prepared for any of her mood changes, last-minute plans, or tirades. He knew what to say and when to say it.

Knowing him so well has made this hard time easier.

She imagines how he would react to her now, through the spectrum of emotions: crying, laughing, frustration, anger, and everything in between. Especially when she snaps at a cabbie, barista, or driver who ran a red light with her usual catchphrase—*"Now what the fuck is this all about?!"*

She looks tenderly at his grave. "I'm hoping there was a

reason for all this. Maybe to save you from a terrible, ugly thing, or to stop a plague, or something else that would save the world."

A gentle gust of wind rustles the branches.

A squirrel scales a tree.

"I start training tomorrow. I may trim my bangs. I'll keep you posted."

Day One, Job One

KATIE HADN'T ASKED Brooke about a dress code, so she just queued off what *she* had worn, then shifted it for someone who was about twenty years younger. Business casual, modest enough, comfortable shoes.

She looks good. Not flashy, not sexy, just professional.

On arrival, she finds Mike waiting. "Good morning, Katie." He has a kind face and looks a little tired. "Cream no sugar, right?" He holds out a paper cup of coffee.

"Hi, yes. How'd you know that?"

He has a firm handshake. "I'm an expert at guessing people's drinks—you should have seen me at the Christmas party."

This is a good start, she thinks. Katie was twenty-two the last time she started a job. That lasted a couple of years before she started freelance designing. She eventually built her own company.

It feels nice to just be taking orders and learning new things. She has no doubt that she'll take over in a year or two. She'll reorganize everything, move Brooke to a significant role on the board, and triple output. But for today, she is the student.

Mike and Katie walk through a foyer into a large open area, reminiscent of an upscale locker room. Shelves are stacked on one side, filled with dark blue jumpsuits. Sizes are noted with small cards tacked to the shelves.

Mike glances at Katie. "Ladies' medium," he says, tossing her a jumpsuit. "Grab yourself a pair of Pumas," he adds, gesturing to another set of shelves.

"Dressing room?" she asks.

"Right behind you."

Weird; she hadn't noticed it on the way in. She prides herself on her powers of observation. First-day jitters, maybe. "I'll be in the foyer. Come on out when you're ready," Mike says. "No rush."

Inside the dressing room, Katie finds a shelf with her name on it. She undresses, stows her things, and slips on the blue jumpsuit. It fits perfectly. She didn't put on socks this morning, but she finds a pair rolled up inside the Pumas.

Standing in front of a full-length mirror, she checks herself out. "I look like a ghostbuster," she muses, smiling. "This is going to be fun."

"You're with me for now," Mike says. "I'm going to be your guide until you're ready to go out on your own."

"Okay."

"It's not a hard job, but the details matter. Are you a details person?"

She is. Details are what made her successful at her own company, and her precision is something she prides herself on. "I am."

His question reinforces Brooke's insistence that she couldn't be more perfect for this job. She appreciates that reinforcement.

"All right, good stuff. So, let me give you the thirty-thousand-foot view." Katie likes big picture discussions. "We get our 'work orders,'" he puts up his fingers in air-quotes, "and follow the instructions. There's a specific order of execution. If you miss a step or do something out of order, or get the *orders* out of order, things can get bad."

"Bad?" She's curious.

"Eh, we'll talk about the 'bad' stuff later. Today, we focus on getting you up to speed so you can start taking on your own 'orders'—deal?"

"Yessir, it's a deal," says the student.

* * *

Mike and Katie emerge from the subway stop on 7th Avenue and 19th Street. There's a small parking lot across the avenue and the scent of pizza in the air.

He pulls a few loose sheets of paper from a well-worn leather folder. The pages are typewritten, with an outline on the front and a diagram on the back. He glances at his watch, then at the top sheet. "Come on." They head toward 20th Street. "This is a good one to start with. There's a watch in your pocket—put it on."

Katie reaches into her jumpsuit pocket, and lo and behold, there it is, just like he said. They double-check to make sure their watches are synchronized.

"We're in sync, great. Have a look here," He shows her one of the sheets. "We've got a partner on this one. Look across the street."

A woman in a blue jumpsuit waves at Katie. Katie waves back. She looks familiar—maybe one of the window washers who had blocked the sidewalk on the day Katie headed to the slaughter of her company.

"That's Elle; she's with us."

This is getting interesting, Katie thinks.

"In about forty-five seconds, check your watch. She's gonna start doing her thing."

"Which is?"

"Hang tight. Look over there." He points. "That's Aaron."

Across the way is a man in his forties with a receding hairline and the pinched expression of a New York veteran who never quite got where they thought they would.

He's clearly in a hurry, checking his watch as he hustles toward the traffic light. Stepping off the curb, he scans for an opening in the downtown traffic, ready to dart across 7th Avenue. A Town Car honks.

"Watch Elle, Katie," Mike whispers.

Elle picks up a large piece of cardboard and starts fanning in Aaron's direction.

"Look uptown, there's a bike messenger at 22nd, see 'im?"

A box truck changes lanes; a bike messenger trails the truck. "Yeah." She's feeling nervous excitement. The intense dance of city traffic.

Elle continues to fan. The pedestrian looks over his shoulder.

The bike messenger is pumping furiously.

Katie focuses on the pedestrian as he licks his lips and checks his watch again. She sees his nostrils flare. He looks uptown. His mouth forms the words, *"Ah, screw it."* He turns around and steps toward the pizza place.

The moment he turns away, Katie screams. A taxi smashes into the pole where the pedestrian stood a fraction of a second before. It would have cut him in half. The bike messenger swerves; a bus slams on its brakes and skids to a stop. "The cab!" She starts to make a move to help.

"He's gonna be fine. Let's break this down, okay?"

"We have to help!"

Katie is speechless, sweating, her heart is racing. A crowd gathers around the crashed taxicab. The cabbie steps out—he IS fine—and Katie is left trying to get out some words.

She grabs Mike's arm. "How?"

"Let's get a slice and talk about it," he says.

The walk east on 20th Street takes them past a little park, a play area for young kids. They sit on a bench with their slices.

"Is this a 'normal' day, would you say?" Katie asks.

"Slow day," he says, working on a bite of pizza.

"That was intense."

"You get used to it."

A rubber ball is rolling toward them, a kid chasing it. Mike picks up the ball and tosses it over the fence into the street. It bounces once, and then a taxi runs over it with a loud pop. The kid starts to cry.

"Had to be done," he says, putting a checkmark on one of the orders in his leather fold. "You okay?"

She nods.

"So," he flips the pizza box over and pulls out a black marker. "Elle is here," he draws the intersection and some X's and arrows on the box, "to help Aaron, who moves from that corner," he draws an arrow, "because the pizza smells so good.

"Because of that, Aaron does not get hit by the cab," he draws a circle around one of the X's, "and that diverts the bike messenger, who avoids getting crushed by the bus— *and* the package he's got will be delivered." He draws a smiley next to the bike messenger. "It's a ripple, a huge ripple—a win, win, win—neat huh?"

"Holy shit," she gasps.

"Right?!"

Katie is in awe. She stammers, "H-h-how did you know?"

Mike has heard this question before. He remembers asking it to Brooke, what seems like centuries ago. Everyone he has ever trained has asked, and the answer frustrates most people.

We Just Know

OF ALL THE first days Katie has ever had, this one ranks only behind her wedding day. She is running on adrenaline. She still can't believe Mike's answer to her question.

"How did you know?" she had asked.

"We just know," he'd said. Hardly an answer.

At the end of her day, she skips out the office door, ready to board any Manhattan-bound train at the 39th Avenue station.

"But how the hell do you know!" she blurts out, still confused. An old woman on the street takes a wide berth around her. A young mother steers her stroller away.

Everything looks different on the way home. The world is a brighter place.

These people have no idea what's going on in the world. Her eyes meet those of an old Asian man and he winks at her. *Is he "one of us?"* she wonders. Then he winks at another woman and licks his lips. Maybe not.

Back on the streets of Manhattan, any worker in a blue jumpsuit is suspect. Linen delivery guy? Window washer?

Garbage collector? Are they all with *The Company*? She needs a drink.

Outside the door of Apartment 4F, Katie fumbles with her keys. Her hands are unsteady, struggling to insert the key into the deadbolt. She takes a deep breath and chuckles. *Zip*—the key slides in. She's almost giddy. She finds the second key for the lock set in the doorknob. *Zip, click, twist.* She's in.

It's quiet in the apartment. She hurries to lock the door behind her, then rushes into her bedroom and launches onto the bed. Face down, she screams into a pillow, then rolls over, spread out in the middle of the bed. "Unbelievable!" The ceiling fan rotates above her.

The hot shower runs over her head for several long minutes, washing away the frenetic energy of the intense day. She breathes in the steamy air and closes her eyes. *This has been the weirdest day of my life*, she thinks. "Without a doubt," she audibly completes the thought.

Katie sips a beer in her white terry cloth robe and fuzzy slippers as she sorts the mail at the kitchen table. There's a letter for John from a finance company with an offer of credit.

The sounds of the city creep through the closed window—two people argue, a distant siren wails, car horns beep in a chaotic symphony, a subway train rumbles and squeals far underground.

Katie replays the day in her head, thinking about the pizza box and Mike explaining it like a high school football coach. She needs to talk to someone.

* * *

"Hello?" on the receiver.

"Brooke, it's Katie."

"I heard about your day. The first one can be a little wild; are you okay?"

Katie doesn't know, and that's exactly what she says. She says it was amazing, crazy, even impossible, but there it was, right in front of her eyes. "I can't believe I get PAID for this! Are you kidding me?" She would have done it just for the thrill.

"Are you still wondering if it's *real?*"

The thoughts and feelings come rapid-fire. The idea crosses Katie's mind that it might all be some kind of complicated con game. She feels nervous about getting sucked into something illegal.

"Con game?" Brooke laughs. "I love your imagination."

"It's beyond that—imagination. I can't—couldn't imagine—how can—I don't have the words—" Katie takes a breath. "I have to believe my own eyes. It's—"

"It's faith."

It seems insane, but Katie believes her.

"Mind blown?"

"Yeah," Katie whispers. She pauses for a long moment. "I'll see you tomorrow. I can't wait."

Not the kind of "influencer" she imagined.

There's a knock at her door.

"Who is it?"

"Courier, ma'am. Package for Katherine Paulson." Katie opens the door with the chain on.

"Hi. Sign here, please." He extends a manila envelope. She looks at the recipient, *Beneficiary of Jonathan Paulson,* and then at the messenger. It's the bike messenger from the accident scene.

"Thanks," she says as she takes it and uncomfortably closes the door. A moment later, she rips open the envelope. Inside is a 500,000-dollar check from John's life insurance.

* * *

Across town, Brooke toys with the telephone on her desk. The look on her face is one of relief, satisfaction, accomplishment—she's smiling on the inside. She glances across the dark oak shelves lining three walls of her study, crammed with books, papers, and folios. Managed chaos. A large table at the center of the room serves as a repository for whatever doesn't fit on the shelves. She closes a folio laid out on the table, reorganizing some loose, yellowed pages. The folio slides back into its slot on the shelf. She closes a heavy, worn book and places it next to another, even more weathered volume. She then peels a sticky note from the table and pins it to the treasure map (crime scene) collage on the fourth wall. She steps back. Then another step.

She inspects the wall—the papers, the notes, the strings connecting everything. The handwritten annotations pinned to papers and photos. "Finally," she says.

The last note she pinned has two words: *"Bike Messenger."*

Frosted Glass Doors

Tuesday: "What's an FGD?"

"There," he points across the office. "Frosted Glass Doors, FGD's."

He's looking over the morning paperwork. "I forgot, this is your first one."

They step through FGD Number 23. "Just stand for a second," Mike says. They wait for the door to close behind them. The moment it does, the ground shimmies like a small earthquake, accompanied by a very quiet mechanical clicking.

All the sounds of the city disappear. "Okay, we're good."

They stand in a long corridor with a window a dozen meters away. It's humid. Her jumpsuit feels heavy.

"What's that sound?"

"Cicadas."

"The bugs?"

"Yep."

A few steps down the corridor, she hears running water, and someone is singing. It sounds like a Tony Bennett song.

They step closer. Condensation is gathered on the window. Heavier drops descend in miniature rivers down the other side of the glass.

The singing gets louder. The song is Tony Bennett's "Rags to Riches." She and John danced to it at their wedding. Their first dance.

They stop and stand at the glass. Someone is singing in the shower.

"Where are we?" she asks.

"New Orleans."

"Louisiana?"

He smiles at her. "Sometimes we travel better than first class."

Katie covers her mouth, stifling a giddy laugh. "I've always wanted to go to New Orleans." (She and John had canceled two attempts to go to Jazz Fest because of work conflicts.)

"What is this place?" she whispers.

He wipes his hand down the sweaty window, clearing some of the condensation. But it's not a window; it's the other side of a mirror.

"It's the other side of a mirror," he says.

Their two faces peer through the mirror into a steamy bathroom—someone is taking a shower.

"Learn Portuguese," says Mike.

"What?"

"Not you, him. They need to move to Brazil. His granddaughter needs to be there—she finds an herb in the Amazon that leads to a cure for diabetes. Amazon Rainforest." He points to the work order. "You wanna do one?"

"Can he hear us?" she asks.

"Depends." He explains that today, these are subliminal messages. This kind of thing happens all the time.

He points to something on the sheet and nods to Katie.

"Brazil nuts," she says, and shrugs with nervous excitement.

"Rio de Janeiro," he says.

The man sticks his head through the opening of the shower curtains. "Honey, how do you feel about South America? I just thought of something."

"His granddaughter finds an herb?" Katie asks. "Do you know what it is?"

"No, it doesn't work that way."

How does *it work?* she thinks.

Katie bounds through Frosted Glass Door Number 23 and back into the office, bursting with the pride of a job well done and the adrenaline rush of a new discovery. She claps her hands and paces like a coach motivating an athlete. "Oh my God, what's next? That was amazing."

Mike remembers being that excited. It's been a while.

"Today? I'm done. We've been gone for fourteen hours."

She looks out the window; the sun is well beyond the horizon, the city is lit up. *"Time will slow down for you,"* Brooke had said.

"Fourteen hours? It seemed like minutes."

"Travel takes time." Mike yawns. "I need to wrap up the paperwork. Good job today." He plants himself in a cubicle and begins to log some of the details of today's job. "Good night."

His "good night" feels more like "go home." "Good night," she says. "See you tomorrow."

At forty-two, work had always been about one thing: a way to fund life. Her father's words, *"Find something you're good at and do it. Just be sure you can support yourself,"* echo in her mind. She hadn't realized work could be this exciting, or even be exciting at all.

As she stands at the office door, ready to leave, she glances in his direction. His eyes are focused on his work, the desk lamp casting the only light in the room. *A little lonely*, she thinks. If they aren't out on orders, he's always there—head down, on the job. The door closes behind her.

Mike hears the pneumatic hiss of the office door, then a soft double-click as it closes. Katie's steps recede, and the elevator announces its arrival with a soft chime. He's alone. Mike likes the solitude. He's used to being alone. The room has a different sound without footsteps, rustling papers, or voices. He opens a drawer on his desk. An orange jostles into view. He takes a minute to peel it; it smells good. He squeezes the rind under his nostrils. The delicate spray of the oils fills his senses. He takes a deep breath. Not too many things are better than a good orange.

Just eat a couple of sections, then back to work, he thinks. He has to finish Katie's performance report. "Helpful? *Check.* Curious? *Check.* Follows orders? *Check.*"

On the sheet is a space for additional comments. He taps his clear, hexagonal, black-ink Bic pen, thinking. He finally writes, *"I know she's been through a lot, but you know what I like about her? She's committed, I think—and seems like she's having fun. I'm used to people ~~kinda~~ going through the motions. We're all so used to it—I guess I'd say she's refreshing."*

What they did today was a Tier One job, meaning it was of significant importance. She handled it well. She'll have one of her own soon.

He smiles with the satisfaction of a good teacher, or a big brother.

Mike double-checks that every aspect has been completed successfully. All the boxes are checked. He signs at the bottom of the page in the space marked *"Supervisor's Signature."*

Done for the day.

With the desk lamp off, the city lights are captivating. They reflect in his tired green eyes.

Mike steps through Frosted Glass Door Number Two and waits for it to close behind him. The moment it does, the rattle of an elevated train thunders around him. He pushes through another door directly in front of him and enters a one-room apartment. A bare fluorescent bulb flickers on with a buzz.

The room is well-kept and clean, but very lived-in. The paint looks like it's from the last century. Cracks mar the glass of the two windows that look out onto the Manhattan Bridge.

An ambulance races across the bridge, its lights filling the room.

A few pictures and paintings hang on one wall, all featuring the same two people—Mike and Brooke.

His clothes hang neatly from a thick dowel roughly nailed into a corner. A single bed is pushed against the wall near the entrance, and a tub rests against the opposite wall. A hot plate and toaster rest on a small table with one chair, next to an ancient refrigerator.

He puts an orange section on the floor next to the fridge. A brown mouse emerges and looks to Mike. "Hi little buddy." The mouse picks up the orange section and gnaws on the edge.

Inside the fridge, a grocery bag is stapled shut with Mike's name written on it in black marker. He tears it open and checks the contents: two paper-wrapped sandwiches, a half dozen cheese sticks, a large bag of sour cream and chive potato chips, English muffins, two pounds of apples, and a package of softening frozen chicken with mixed vegetables. "Better put those in the freezer."

He pulls out a sandwich, breaks off a piece of the crust, and sets it on the floor for the mouse. "Dinner for two," he says, pulling the chair next to the window.

A train rattles along the tracks under the bridge. It's noisy and barely a stone's throw away.

Below, someone burns garbage and a busted-up pallet in a barrel. Sirens blaze by. Even amidst the chaos and noise of the city, watching the large, soft snowflakes drift down captures Mike's imagination. A few flakes stick to the window, melting into drops that run down the glass and collect at the bottom.

Welcome home.

Hopes and Dreams #1
The Condor

Some of the trees in the Northern California Redwood Forest are more than a thousand years old. It's breathtaking. Today, the sky is a deep blue. Occasional clouds, reminiscent of white spun cotton candy, drift lazily east. The Redwood Forest is home to countless species and, at the right time of year, is deeply serene.

Mike walks among the towering redwoods. Branches rustle in the breeze, while bird calls and animal sounds echo around him. Directly in front of him stands a majestic tree. Its deep auburn bark stretches upward, giving way to powerful boughs and lush greenery.

Overhead, a wild California Condor navigates the canopy. Its unmistakable, immense wingspan casts a shadow on him as it passes. These birds are a rare sight. Its pink head, white markings, and jet black feathers look of previous millennia. The condor glides on the breeze and in for a landing on a mighty bough. As it settles, the weight of the bird begins to strain the tree; the ancient giant starts to lean. Its roots crack and slowly pull from the earth.

Mike watches the tree slowly tip directly toward him.

He smiles at the falling giant and thinks, *I could run, but I'd rather not.* A tear of joy runs down his face.

The tree reaches the floor of the forest with a thunderous crash, its mighty branches flexing on impact. The condor stands on the giant horizontal trunk and walks to the edge. Mike's fingers protrude from under it, the only part of him visible, not crushed by the fall.

The bird jumps down, bites off one of the fingers, and swallows it with a guttural honk.

Back in New York City, Mike's head rests on his pillow. He's dead asleep and grinning from ear to ear.

Saint Malo to Liverpool

1891

France

THE MASTS of the tall sailing ships sway gently in the harbor in Saint Malo, France. It's a bustling port city near the Atlantic, at the southern end of the English Channel.

The woman and the boy were ordered there two years ago. "Endless travel," the boy calls it.

Some days, he is allowed to go out on his own. "It's all right to observe, but do not initiate conversations or give answers to questions. If someone asks a question, you must say, 'I'm sorry, I don't know.' Do you understand?"

"I understand," he says.

He loves watching the West African men working on the docks—powerful, productive, free. They help load wine and textiles onto ships bound for America, and they unload ivory and gold from Africa, or sugar and tobacco from the Caribbean—and they look like him.

"What do you want, boy?" one of them asks.

The boy had been concealing himself behind a stack of

wooden pilings on the dock as he watched them unload shipments of tobacco from Virginia in the New World. The Black men on the ship are lifting bales of the sweet-smelling leaves and dropping them onto a wagon. The French love the American tobacco; the smell of it burning is everywhere in the city.

"I'm sorry, I don't know," says the boy, and he runs off.

But he *does* know. He wants this kind of work—working to make tangible things happen. He wants to be like the rest of them. He wants to eat wonderful food, help build beautiful buildings, and sail the seas to see the world in a new way. He can, however, only watch. They will not work with him, a boy of eleven or twelve.

He is, of course, not eleven or twelve, but he looks it. It has been more than one hundred years since he was taken from Rome. He doesn't know what magic makes him age unlike other people. He has spent many evenings alone in his bed, weeping about it.

On another spring day, a rope hoists wooden boxes onto a ship bound for Canada. The boxes are filled with bottles of wine. A White man, referred to as the "captain," inspects the loading of the ship. He shakes the hand of another White man, congratulating him on the work. The boy hasn't noticed any White men working to load or unload. He hides among stacks of large coiled ropes.

He's hypnotized by a world unknown to him.

"Boy," a deep voice shakes him out of his trance. "The captain needs a cabin boy."

Standing before him is one of the dockworkers he's been watching wrangle heavy cargo for months. The man is tall, and he's sweaty from the hard labor. His skin is black, his eyes kind, and his voice resonant but quiet. "Can you speak?" he asks.

Telling the man he does not know how to speak, as instructed, will sound foolish. "Yes, I can," he replies.

A slow smile creeps across the man's face. "Can you work? Have you been to sea? In two days, we sail for Quebec City. You'll return in five months with fur and wheat and a pocket full of francs."

Five months on the open ocean, across the world. Learning a real craft, working with real people. The boy tries to conceal his excitement, but his mind is racing with possibilities, and his heart races with anticipation. He forgets about his current situation as a nomad, year after year, living a life with no answers. Being bound to youth and bound to the woman. Being a prisoner.

He wants to say yes to this man. To an introduction to the captain. To set foot onto the ship. His face cannot hide any of it. His eyes are desperate to hold back the moisture collecting in them, knowing he must ask permission, and what his next words must be.

* * *

"But why not!?" he bellows to the woman, his caretaker, the one he calls "Mama." She explains in detail, despite his furious protests and desperate reasoning. He begs, but the answer remains unchanged.

And now, again, they will leave.

"We must go to England," she says.

He weeps at those words. He has heard them dozens of times before, but never with such prospects before him. His anger swells. His protests grow more absolute, but to no avail.

On a cold October morning, they arrive at the docks as passengers with one large trunk and two small bags. *Take only what you must,"* the order says. The morning mist drifts across the damp wooden dock; the gangplank glistens with dew. Try as it might, the sun fails to break through the low clouds. Tall, muscular West African men load their possessions into the ship's hold. The boy begs her to stay. The answer is the same as it has been every time he has asked during the fourteen days since she first told him. "There is a task of major importance for something in the next century. We must go."

"The next century? How can we know!?" he cries.

"We just know," she says.

He has heard this infuriating answer before, usually followed by "have faith."

"And this task is in England?"

"No, it's aboard this ship." She explains: the task is his. He's to steal two bottles of liquor from the captain's quarters and toss them overboard. If he does, the captain will not become drunk and fall asleep. The ship will not collide unnoticed with a smaller vessel. The captain of that smaller vessel, who is an engineer, a scientist, and a shipbuilder, will survive. He will go on to work on an unsinkable titan of a transatlantic steamship. This titan will transport a young girl, and her descendant will hold the key to research that can save the planet.

"The entire planet?" he says. "Why is it up to us to save the planet? That should be the job of kings and queens and noblemen."

"It isn't. It is ours, but not ours alone. There are others. All around the world."

This is actually comforting to him; they are not alone.

"Can I meet them?"

"You will—at the right time. This is what they told me. But I don't know when that is."

And so she tells him about the couple who knocked on the door in Paris. That they knew about every task they had done and every one they failed to do. She can't bear to tell him the extent of the damage; he is just a boy. *Tell him enough to make him see the importance*, she thinks. A boy doesn't need to know such tragedy exists in the world.

His anger quiets, he listens; he comes to understand.

The excitement that had been on the boy's face and the dreams that had been in his heart are extinguished.

She shows him a drawing: two lines that meet at the bottom of the paper, in the shape of a cone. At the intersection of the lines is a date and time of day. Between the lines are numbered dots; outside the lines are dots with letters. She explains it is a map of sorts, showing what might happen when they do their tasks. World events, good or bad, can be triggered based on what they do. So they must be precise and careful not to do it poorly.

After all this time, this is the first meaning assigned to what they have been doing. *Is there a plan?* the boy wonders.

The three-day journey from Saint Malo to Liverpool begins. The seas are exceptionally rough, and the boy becomes exceptionally sick. On the second evening, he needs to complete his task. Blinded by nausea, his attempt to break into the captain's cabin is unsuccessful. He stumbles into that of the first officer by mistake and dumps the wrong liquor. Because of the captain's drinking, the collision with the smaller craft happens. The engineer does not get hired by Harland & Wolff in Northern Ireland. As a result, the ship Harland & Wolff is going to build does not benefit from his knowledge of secondary double-walled chambers and sinks after a collision with an iceberg. The ship is the *Titanic*. This event is one of the worst maritime tragedies in the history of the world.

An unexpected consequence of this failure is that a boy named Ivan Vaughan will introduce two young musicians at a summer church event in the Woolton neighborhood of Liverpool, England: John Lennon and Paul McCartney. They will eventually form The Beatles and entertain billions.

FACTS ABOUT
CONE DIAGRAMMES

Every task & order comes with a cone-shaped diagramme.

Two lines make up the cone and
meet near the bottom of the page.

That intersection is the moment
that the order ought to be fulfilled.

Based on how exact that timing is, the (significant) occurrences
noted within the cone are possible (significant) outcomes.

Occurrences outside the cone are undesirable.

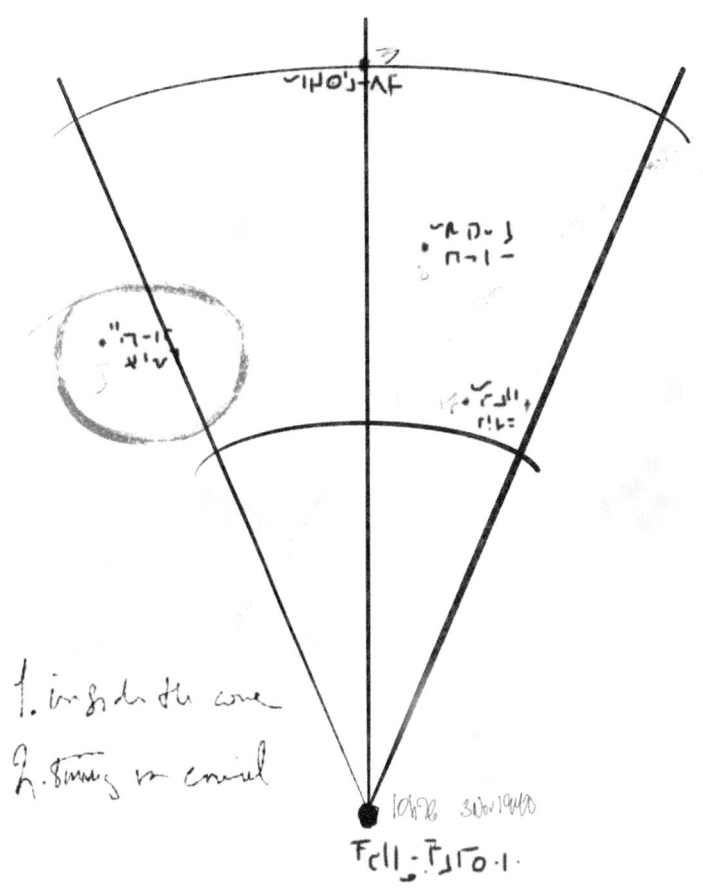

1. inside the cone

2. staying on central

fig. 001a   Cone Diagramme

Official Junior Influencer

THE WEATHERMAN on the radio says rain is expected this evening. It's Wednesday in an overcast and breezy Williamstown, Massachusetts. Katie sits on a curb and holds a rag and a bamboo skewer. There's no foot traffic. She unfolds the paper containing the order for this job and confirms her location—Park Street.

Just as the order states: *"Brown Town Car, Maine license plates, Grateful Dead stickers on the back window."* Katie glances up and down the block and checks over her shoulder. Other than a feral cat and a retiree on a recumbent bicycle, the coast is clear. She unscrews the valve stem cap on the right rear tire. After a last look around, she jams the bamboo skewer into the valve. The compressed air begins its exodus. She twists the skewer in with enough force to make it stick. The swish of air rushing out of the tire smells stale and feels cold. She imagines the escaping air is happy to be free, and back in the outside world. Slowly, the rear of the Town Car begins to sink as the tire loses its shape and goes flat. She walks away and wipes black soot from her fingers with the rag. The bamboo skewer remains, protruding from the valve.

According to the cone diagram, letting the air out of the car's tire will delay the driver—a janitor named Phil, who's employed at St. John's Episcopal Church—in picking up his aunt, a retired general practitioner named Ruth, who is supposed to be traveling via Greyhound bus on the 8:20 a.m. from Pittsfield to Boston. She would then connect to another bus to Woods Hole and a ferry to Martha's Vineyard. Because of the delay, she will have to take the afternoon train instead (as there's only one bus a day from Pittsfield to Boston). She will miss the connecting bus in Boston and will have to hire a car to make the drive to Woods Hole, hoping to catch the last ferry to the island.

Due to this change, she will be first on the scene of a four-car pile-up on I-495 near Middleborough and save the life of a teenager—a teenager who will eventually lead a research team at Princeton that creates an optic nerve repair process capable of reversing the effects of severe degenerative eye diseases.

Friday: Tucson, Arizona. Katie puts fifty cents in an expired parking meter in the one hundred block of South 6th Avenue. The parking enforcement woman giving out tickets won't have to stop to issue a citation.

Because of that, she will not get caught at a red light, will not be delayed by the minor accident that occurs about sixty seconds after she passes through the intersection, and will make it to her daughter's school play just as her kid comes on stage. Her daughter will witness her mother brimming with pride, howling and clapping loudly.

Thanks to her mother's encouragement at that moment, she will go on to pursue her dream of stage acting, get accepted with a full scholarship to the prestigious Yale Drama School, and begin a Broadway career right out of college. She will win a Tony Award for her first role and eventually use her good fortune for philanthropy, raising millions for charity.

* * *

Monday: Near Carampoma, Peru. Katie and Mike go through another Frosted Glass Door. "Why so early?" she asks as she looks at the order and her watch.

"Eh, it's gonna take a few minutes to get used to the altitude."

The base of the mountain is 11,181 feet above sea level.

"What's in the suitcase?"

"Costumes."

They arrive in a small meadow 12,481 feet above sea level; it's cold and sunny. Something between a breeze and a wind blows. Katie takes a deep breath. "The air."

"Smells better than New York in the summer, doesn't it?"

Somewhere, someone has a wood fire burning. That scent coasting on the breeze reminds her of the late summer of her tenth year at Laurel Lake. Katie and her mother collected long twigs and whittled the ends clean and sharp. Then they sat around the stone fire pit on the teak benches her grandfather made to roast marshmallows.

Mike kneels and unzips the ivory-colored Samsonite suitcase. He unclips the straps that bind its contents and hands her a tan fuzzy jumpsuit. It has a hood with a lion's mane, and on the rear, a long tail.

"Really?" Katie remembers something similar from her junior high school trick-or-treating days.

"Suit up."

At twelve thousand feet above sea level, if you're not used to it, it's easy to get winded. Katie realizes she's out of breath as she steps into the jumpsuit. "This altitude is no joke."

"Stay in the game. This is Tier One. Are you ready?"

"As I'll ever be." She attempts a deep inhale through her nostrils, then again through her mouth as they take a few steps. They reach the apex. It's one of the most beautiful places Katie has ever seen: snowy peaks, green fields, a clear blue lake, and a small herd of sheep with a shepherd. *Amazing that this exists today*, she thinks, being used to the concrete jungle of New York City.

"Let's go. Make it loud."

"What?"

"Do what I do."

Mike takes off running toward the herd of sheep, his hands in the air. He's doing the worst impression of a lion imaginable. "Raarrrr! Rooaaaar!" Katie follows suit.

The sheep instinctually, almost in unison, raise their heads from nibbling grass. There are predators (in fuzzy tan lion suits) coming. The frantic bleating from the sheep, due to the perceived danger, sends them into a stampede. The shepherd, certain that his eyeglasses need to be replaced, runs after them, trying to calm the herd. They are moving fast. Instinct has taken over.

A moment later, there's an earthy rumble. Birds take flight. The ground shifts under their feet. The few trees that exist at twelve thousand feet violently sway. The sheep continue their stampede. A major earthquake is happening exactly along the ridge that the sheep and the shepherd occupied only a moment ago. The patch of long, swaying grass begins to tear. A tree snaps like a twig; sharp rocks crack and push their way through the opening in the ground. The crack widens into a chasm in a matter of seconds. The ground rips open like a bag of chips. The shepherd stumbles and regains his footing. The sheep run, bleating and screeching. As the rumble slows, so do the sheep. They begin to find each other and reconvene. The shepherd huffs and limps to his herd, looking back at the chasm they narrowly escaped from. The massive crack in the earth would have consumed them, burying them alive and crushing them into pulp. The shepherd kneels and prays.

Mike and Katie stop, gasping for air. She falls to her knees.

"Oh—my—what?" She can't get another word out. No oxygen.

They both lie on their backs, pulling deep breaths. They can see their breath against the shocking blue of the sky. Two small aftershocks shake the hillside.

"The shepherd needs to survive," Mike wheezes. "Tonight, he will father a significant person."

"Who?"

"A little girl with something special in her genes," he says, out of breath and with a deep look of satisfaction. "The kid will be the cure for cancer."

* * *

Wednesday: Heavy black cables hang behind Mike and Katie. Somewhere nearby, in this cavernous room, an intermittent rumble is followed by a wheezing rush of air. Katie has never seen any place like it. "Where are we?"

He raises a finger to his lips. She understands.

They walk on a wooden platform in a darkened, rectangular tunnel, open at both ends. The grain on the wood looks foreign and artificial, with large, long, sweeping curves. A few steps ahead on the platform, where the tunnel ends, she can see two large yellowed circles, either worn into the platform or painted on. The rumble and the wheeze get louder. There is a dropoff ahead; the platform ends.

Katie is startled by a loud crinkling noise and quickly covers her mouth to stifle a reflexive gasp. Something massive is moving in front of them. She grabs Mike's arm. "It's okay," he whispers. A human hand, the size of a compact car, drops in front of them. The tips of the fingers graze the wooden floor and flex. A giant person momentarily wakes, then falls back asleep. The wheeze turns into a choke and then into a snore.

She frantically whispers into Mike's ear, "What is going on?!" Katie can now see the giant in full length. It's wearing a white t-shirt and pajama bottoms. The giant's head is immense, its bald spot expansive. It's asleep on a couch that appears to be the size of a small office building. Katie looks above her head; there's a lamp, with a chain hanging next to a lightbulb that looks big enough to crush them both. "Are we on another world?"

"Watch, this is the fun part."

"But...."

It's too late; he hops from the wooden floor onto the massive sofa. Katie feels panic setting in—they're going to be crushed. Mike creeps next to the giant's ear. He slips as he climbs a giant pillow but steadies himself and *winks* at her. *He's lost it*, she thinks. Mike then whispers something and quickly jumps back to the wooden platform. *It's an end table!* she realizes. The yellowed rings are water stains from a giant glass of ice water. The cables are the cords for the lamp and the clock that stand next to it.

The giant wakes with a shriek, screams a deafening scream, and starts slapping itself in the face.

Socializing

LAUGHTER CAN BE HEARD behind Frosted Glass Door Number 18. It flies open.

"What did you say?" she asks, but he's laughing uncontrollably.

She punches him in the arm. "What did you say?!" But it's that crazy kind of laughter that just won't stop. The moment it subsides, another wave hits. A cathartic release. Katie hasn't seen him enjoy himself this much the entire time they've worked together.

"They look just like humans! Where were we? Are there giants?"

He chokes out, through the last moments of laughter, "Far Rockaway. Oh, man. That felt good."

"Far Rockaway?"

"Sometimes we get small—depending on the job. He's not a giant." A residual chuckle escapes. "I told him there was a spider on his face."

"Won't there be repercussions from that?"

"You mean in the grand scheme of things?"

She nods.

"No, Tier Four jobs are just for fun—they have zero effect on anything else. Sometimes you just gotta let off some steam, you know?"

Yet another day of surprises, Katie thinks as she finishes up the day's paperwork. She has to laugh as she recalls the job—or, not really a job; more like a therapy session. *We all need to blow off some steam from time to time.* She looks at the clock. It's closing time.

"Let's go grab a beer and shoot the shit for a bit," she says.

Mike stays focused on his paperwork. "No, I don't do that."

This is the first job she's ever had with absolutely no casual interaction. No after-work cocktails or personal chit-chat with coworkers.

"Why not?" Katie asks.

He rests his pen on the desk and leans back in his chair, bracing for the conversation.

"I don't socialize—with people—in public. And I have a pet at home that needs feeding."

"What kind of pet? Bird? Cat?"

"No, not one of those."

"Is it going to die if you're not home for an hour?"

"You never know."

"A puppy? A snake?"

"No."

"You're not the best at small talk."

"I know."

"Come on. We already spend hours together traveling and hanging out. This will be just like that, except without the work orders—one drink, on me! Get to know each other a little—make a new friend?"

"I've never done that."

"You've never gone out for a drink?"

"I've never made a friend."

That's about the saddest sentence Katie has ever heard. *He's serious*, she thinks. She doesn't know where she'd be now without her close friends, especially after all that's happened.

She owes it to him to let him know he's wrong. "Mike Romano of New York City, you *have* made a friend. And this friend is going to buy you an Old Fashioned."

* * *

The lighting in the Irish pub near 31st and Broadway in Queens occasionally flickers. It's a dim, dingy, hole-in-the-wall pub.

Regulars perch at the end of the bar, baseball caps and down vests still dirty from the day. It's not a place anyone would take a date, but it's perfect for an after-work drink.

"...she's got a million stories. One time when I was little," Mike is a little tipsy, "she said that I messed up some Tier One job and John Wilkes Booth was my fault."

"Is that right?" Katie laughs. "Where were you during the Civil War?"

"England, I think, but this was the late 1840s." He raises a finger to the bartender. "One more round."

Katie, entertained by this yarn, encourages him on. "Of course, do tell."

He leans in, and in a very serious tone whispers, "I had to pee really bad. Because of that, we missed a boat, and because of that and a couple other things, little Mr. Booth got born."

There's an old-fashioned record-spinning jukebox at the far end of the bar. "Please, Mr. Postman" by The

Marvelettes starts playing. Mike hops up from his stool and starts singing along. "Do you know this song?"

She does. "Written by Georgia Dobbins and Bill Garrett."

"You're good. Do you know how it got to Berry Gordy of Motown Records?"

"I wasn't born yet!"

"Yours truly," he proudly says.

The bartender arrives with fresh Old Fashioneds.

"And who do you think planted the seeds for the idea of the Underground Railroad to free the slaves?"

"You?"

"That's right. What about the Macarena?"

"I'm guessing you," she says. They sing a few bars and go through the motions of the Macarena.

"You know, it's nice that all this stuff is gonna happen the way it's supposed to—people talk, and the Universe listens." He grabs his drink. "We don't get it right all the time, like war and disease and stuff—but here's to the grand plan." He raises his glass.

"Here's to you, my friend." Katie clinks his glass.

The evening goes on, and the stories and the booze and the good vibes keep flowing.

They laugh, they tell secrets, they shoot the shit. Each learns a little bit about the other.

They become friends.

A Good Morning

EARLY IN SPRING, before the leaves in the trees return, the east-facing windows of Apartment 4F get the morning sun.

Katie is usually an early riser, but not today. When her eyes open, memories of blurry college life return. This is her first hangover in twenty years.

She coughs out a chuckle. It was a truly good time last night, the first one in a while. Loosening up enough to truly enjoy herself has been difficult because John's passing lingers in most of her actions and colors everyday life. She knows he will always be there, but she also feels a little more free this morning, like a hurdle has been overcome.

However, she is a little queasy. Might be time for some toast. A glass of water, or maybe juice. She is definitely dehydrated. As soon as she opens the fridge, she turns and runs for the toilet and throws up.

"Oh, that was not fun," she mumbles. Katie rinses the tangy bile out of her mouth and fumbles her way to the couch. She has the chills. She wraps herself up in a crocheted afghan and covers her head with a pillow.

In Katie's dream, she can hear someone banging on the

wall. *No more mixing drinks*, she thinks. The banging stops, and then light hits her eyes; someone has pulled the pillow away from her face. Katie wakes, groggy and confused.

"I thought we were brunching," says Shelby, who hovers over Katie in her compromised state.

"Hi." Katie manages, "I'm not so sure about that. I may have been drinking last night."

"You look pretty green." Shelby helps her to sitting. "What say we get you a B12 shot and then some eggs Benedict?"

"Let's not talk about food, please," Katie says as she pushes her way past Shelby to throw up again. Shelby follows. She's the friend who holds your hair when you barf. "I think that's all of it."

But Katie was wrong. The next morning, she had a similar episode, but hadn't had anything to drink. Not even a mimosa at brunch. Then once more in the middle of the night and again the following morning.

* * *

"Good morning—Katie?" There's a new receptionist at Katie's general practitioner. "I've got your paperwork," she says, handing her a clipboard. "And when you're done, see if you can fill this up for me." She puts a sticker with Katie's information onto a plastic urine sample container. "Thanks!"

Cheery, Katie thinks.

After taking care of the urine business, Katie waits on the paper-covered exam bench. Her feet dangle above the step.

"How are we this morning, Mrs. Paulson?"

"Where's Doctor Amy?"

"Bermuda for two weeks. I'm afraid you're stuck with me. I'm Doctor Lee."

He extends his hand, and she accepts it. "Nice to meet you."

Doctor Amy has been Katie's person since she was a teenager. She's been there for every dramatic event in her life since those years. Katie explains about the vomiting and the hangover, adding that it's been about twenty years since her last bender.

"Let's start with some simple stuff," Doctor Lee says, taking out a notepad. "How about some B6 supplements, once a day for the rest of the week, and some good old Pepto-Bismol? If you're not feeling considerably better by tomorrow night, we can take some blood and see where things go."

"Seems like sound advice."

"It's going to be fine, Katie. Probably just a reaction to a little too much bourbon."

"That's a good guess."

"Really nice to meet you. And if anything comes up in the urine test, I'll give you a call."

She *does* feel better by the next afternoon. Not one hundred percent, but better. Until Doctor Lee calls.

Central Park is dusted with fresh snow. There aren't too many people milling around the Mall today—much of it is blissfully unscathed by footprints.

Katie sits on a bench and watches the world go by. *The mind-blowing continues*, she thinks. A few fluffy flakes land on her face. She sticks out her tongue and catches a few more.

Katie made one phone call after hearing from the doctor.

"Okay, what's the big news?" Shelby calls from a few feet away.

The few pedestrians on the Mall witness the spectacle of two women laughing, crying, screaming, and holding hands while jumping in a circle. "Pregnant! Oh my God! We're having a baby!" Neither can contain themselves.

When the laughing, crying, screaming, and hopping subsides, they plop down on the bench. "This changes everything!" Shelby howls. "We have shopping to do, painting to do, and—names! What are we going to name her?"

This is the best response Katie could have imagined.

"So you're in, Shelby? Mother's little helper?"

"Are you kidding? Of course! I'm finally going to be an aunt!"

Visit to John

AT THE CROWDED N R subway stop at NYU, Katie leans against the white and tan tile wall. It's her first solo Tier One job. The downtown N train is arriving. It's 5:24 pm, right on schedule. A cacophony of sound, and a river of people exiting in an orderly fashion.

Katie is thinking of John for this one; it's a very "him" thing to do.

Per unwritten New York subway rules, the passengers on the train exit first. People stream off the train: a baby boomer with a ten-speed, college kids in a cluster, academic types working on paperbacks or the crossword.

The crowd starts to board; there's plenty of room on the train. Katie checks her watch and looks to the stairs from the street. A pair of feet rushes down.

"Stand clear of the closing doors," says the conductor. The doors click open, then the chimes sound again. The person who was rushing down the stairs is now at the turnstile.

"Whoever is blocking the doors, stand clear."

She's through the turnstile.

"Stop blocking the doors, people!"

The late passenger jumps through an open door and Katie lets the door close. The important passenger is aboard. Job complete.

Hearing the conductor of the train chastise whoever was blocking the door makes Katie giggle.

It's amazing, she thinks, *how little things can make a difference.*

If the running woman missed the train, she would have been late to a job interview. She would have failed to get the job, and its paycheck. Unable to pay the rent, she'd be evicted from her apartment. Their special needs kid would have been yanked from a school they were getting great benefits from.

* * *

"This is a multi-level gag," Mike says. "Two Tier Ones combined."

This is a first, Katie thinks.

"The order says there's going to be a fire."

It's a late afternoon filled with dark, heavy clouds. They're on 41st Street between Greenpoint and Queens Boulevard in Sunnyside, Queens. A mix of single-family homes and small three- and four-story apartment buildings line the block.

High winds blow in ahead of a thunderstorm expected in the next twelve hours. Branches rustle aggressively. Newspaper pages and leaves swirl in mini-tornadoes, and a candy wrapper blows across the street.

A glow comes from the windows of most of the residences on the block; it's dinner time. Aside from three kids on scooters at the end of the block, the sidewalk is empty.

"Can you pull a brick from that garden, please?"

"Sure. Sorry, petunias." Katie removes a brick from a handmade miniature flower garden between the sidewalk and the curb. "What are we doing?"

"The fire is going to be in one of those." Mike indicates two identical (but mirrored) four-story buildings. "There is one fire hydrant on this block, and that," he points to a rusty green Pontiac, "is blocking it."

"One sec." Mike takes out his phone and dials 911. He suddenly sounds frantic. "There's a fire! 41st Street, north of 48th Ave! Oh my, hurry!" He hangs up.

"What was that about?"

Mike looks at his watch.

Just then, a gust of wind blows by, and a loud crack sounds from a nearby maple tree. A heavy bough falls against a power line. The line snaps, and the cable whips against a window and shatters it. Drapes in the broken window ignite—polyester likes to burn. The transformer on the pole blows with a sharp boom and a blinding flash.

"Can I have that, please?" Mike takes the brick and throws it through the window of the Pontiac. He pulls a screwdriver and wire cutter from the pocket of his jumpsuit, then lets himself into the car and, like an expert thief, hot-wires it in less than ten seconds.

People are streaming onto the street. Fire trucks tear around the corner at Greenpoint Avenue.

"Where did you learn to do...?"

The engine revs, the rear tires scream, and a moment later Mike skids the car into an open driveway. Katie appears at the broken window a moment later. He looks past her, and she follows his gaze. The fire truck pulls up to the hydrant that the rusty Pontiac was just blocking.

Mike extracts himself from the car. "Go tell a fireman

there's a deaf woman in 3R; she's pregnant. Her water is about to break—early."

"Oh no." And she's gone.

Mike catches the entertainment section of a *New York Post* dancing in the wind and wipes the shards of broken glass from his clothes.

The street is blocked. Katie lies her way past the tape. "I'm with maintenance," she says. "Let me shut off the building electric." A cop waves her through. Two paramedics stand by, waiting for the "all clear" from the fire department. "Did they tell you guys about the pregnant lady in 3R? She's hard of hearing and may have no idea what's going on," she tells the paramedics.

This changes the calculation. One of the paramedics heads for the fire chief, while the other takes Katie by the arm. "Show me," she says. "Put this on." Katie takes the mask, and they start up the building's rear staircase.

"Fireman!" The paramedic yells down the hall. "I need this door open now!" As the door bursts open, the second paramedic runs onto the third-floor landing. Screams of labor mix with the fire and chaos.

Mike leans against the Pontiac as Katie returns. "They've got her," she says.

"Maintenance crew, nice touch."

"How did you know?"

"We just know," he says with a wink.

A gurney carrying the woman rolls by, a paramedic advising her to breathe and telling her she's going to be fine. The deep groan of a labor pain fills the evening air.

Later that evening, the world will have a new citizen. A little girl with black curly hair and copper skin. Her blue eyes will eventually turn emerald green. She will become a scientist, and her curious and clever mind will take her to Africa. She will devise an incredible plan to create a water distribution system that will save countless people from death and disease. She will become a mother herself and a person of importance at the United Nations. She will change the world.

Because Katie pulled a brick from a petunia garden and Mike moved a rusty Pontiac.

"Let's get something to eat. Iced coffee or something."

"The multi-level ones can stress you out." *She looks a little pale*, he thinks.

"Bodega," Katie says.

A few minutes later, Katie is in possession of a paper sack—two Italian subs and a bag of Funyuns. She knows this neighborhood; it's not far from John in the Calvary Cemetery. "Do we have a few minutes for a picnic?" she asks. "I need to tell John something."

"Of course. We're pretty much done for the day."

"It's a ten-minute walk to the Queens Boulevard entrance. You should come say hi."

"Sure."

The original name of the neighborhood was Blissville—now Sunnyside. Ever optimistic in this part of New York.

They pass through the cemetery's iron gate, its rusty bolts driven into the granite fence back in 1848 when it first opened. The cemetery had been necessary because a cholera epidemic filled up the Mulberry Street cemetery in Manhattan. Grave markers large and small rest amongst trees and gentle slopes.

Deep in the massive cemetery is John's marker. *"Husband and Best Friend"* is inscribed on the polished marble face.

"You go ahead," Mike says, respectfully hanging back.

"Sit with me." She hands him a sandwich and rips open the bag of Funyuns. "We ate a lot of Funyuns."

"I feel you. They're delicious."

Katie sits on the cold earth next to John's grave and lays out the sandwich and a handful of Funyuns. Like a picnic on a late summer day.

"So—honey. I have news. I hope this doesn't come as too much of a shock, but you are going to be a father. Your final gift to me."

Mike hands her a napkin, predicting tears on the near horizon.

"I know you can't be here for it, but you will be in my mind for every step. I'm grateful that everything I know about being kind, generous, and creative—and everything else I learned from you—is with me. I know that sometimes I kind of suck and get in a hurry. You were always the voice in my head, and in life, that gave me calm and peace. I will give it to the kid as best I can. Co-parents. Okay?"

Another napkin.

"We will come visit as soon as possible, so he or she will know where you are. We will have a good life, and we will have the best times thanks to all the warmth and wonderfulness that came from you."

She chokes out tears. Mike puts a hand on her shoulder.

"Dammit, I can't believe this. I just want you to know, I'll try to be a good mom, and I'll always be here for the baby."

She is out of words and full of regrets. Birds chatter in a nearby tree, leaves rustle, a squirrel hops by, and somewhere miles away, a siren wails.

Mike's eyes start to tear up. "I'll be here too, Johnny—Uncle Mike will be here as long as I can."

"This is Mike. He's been a good friend."

Little John's Room

IT COULD BE a flashback to their college days. A canvas covers the floor, and empty water bottles and bags of take-out are scattered around.

Katie and Shelby step back to examine a few paint swatches on the wall where the light from the window is best. They hold paint rollers in both hands like gunfighters —yellow, peach, green, violet.

"Let's stick with neutral colors."

"Nothing pink or blue."

They agree on that.

"Are you going to find out the gender?" Shelby asks.

"Probably. I have an appointment in a couple of weeks."

The afternoon drifts through conversations and cups of coffee. They speculate on how gifted the child will be, their favorite color, and when they'll have their first broken heart. They laugh at old stories and joke about old boyfriends.

Katie is crocheting a yellow, green, and red beanie, reggae style. "Whatever sex you choose," she says to her midsection, "your nickname will be 'Little John.'"

Another thing Shelby and Katie agree on.

The co-parenting is going great.

"Do you think this is all part of the grand plan, Shel?"

"What do you mean?"

"John dying, the baby coming, us meeting in eighth grade, that we both like black licorice and anchovies? You think destiny is a thing? You've said it yourself, 'the Universe must be sending a message about'—whatever."

"I think the Universe wants me to stop crocheting." Shelby holds up a clunky-looking strand of yarn.

"One hundred percent."

The Elevator

THE PERSONNEL at the Universe rotate so that no one works more than five days a week. The office is normally open every day, with one exception. On the twenty-second day of every month (today) the office is closed, and the other branches pick up the slack.

Mike steps out through Frosted Glass Door Number 2, wearing a bathrobe, bedroom slippers, and holding a cup of coffee. The office is empty. The door to Brooke's office creaks as he opens it; a dust bunny hops through a sliver of sunlight. He's alone.

The chain across the "Out of Service" elevator is padlocked. Mike counts the links that hang freely after the lock—seven on one side, four on the other. "Seven and four," he mumbles to himself.

He enters the elevator. There is a second door opposite the one he opened, like a freight elevator. The floor selection panel has buttons numbered zero through nine. The first door closes behind him.

Mike presses a sequence of buttons, but the elevator doesn't move. After a metallic groan, the opposite door opens into a pitch black room. A small circle of light comes from inside the elevator, but beyond that, there is only darkness. Mike reaches around a corner and flips a switch. Dozens of large banks of overhead lights clunk on, one after the other.

The cavernous room that is now illuminated looks like a warehouse. Fifty-foot ceilings, a quarter mile long and just as wide. Tall, thin shelves sit about two feet apart in a grid, like a supermarket with very long, narrow aisles.

Mike approaches an old computer setup and blows the dust off the keyboard. He pushes the button to turn the monitor on. It blinks to life, slowly waking like a teenager on a summer day.

A search box appears on the screen with a cursor flashing in a field labeled NAME. He keys in the words, JONATHAN PAULSON. Sounds of whirring and spinning come from all around the massive room, then 31,462 responses pop up. The cursor jumps to another box. The computer prompts: LOCATION. He enters, NEW YORK STATE; 1,487 responses. The next field, DECEASED, has the flashing cursor and the text Y/N. Mike enters what he knows to be true, and the computer responds: DEATH RANGE. Mike keys in, 12 MONTHS. The computer gives a single response with two choices: VIEW and SAVE.

He selects VIEW. A large, twenty-foot tall hologram presents itself and starts to display a series of images. They illuminate Mike's face as would multi-colored strobe lights at New York City's hottest disco. Minutes pass as the parade of images marches before him.

"Stop there," he says as he presses a key. He skillfully taps the keyboard, well-knowing the commands to control this machine. The pictures are no longer flashing. A video plays. Mike sits back in his chair to watch. His eyes brighten, and the corners of his mouth elevate ever so slightly. He can almost feel the light breeze and the sunshine. He can hear the Canadian geese.

He pulls a USB thumb drive from the pocket of his robe and pushes it into a port on the computer.

Disruption

BROOKE IS DISTRACTED. A tall stack of work orders needs attention on her desk, but something on the "treasure map" looks wrong. *Why does this make no sense?* she thinks. *It did yesterday.* She steps to the map, studying it. "Got to keep the train on the tracks."

She moves a green push pin on the wall.

The fibers of the Universe lay out before her, and yet there's still some manual labor involved.

Katie unlocks the door of Apartment 4F. The kitchen light is on—she must have forgotten to turn it off. She's wound up, anxious. A mundane task is exactly what she needs right now.

She drops some mail on the kitchen table: a credit card offer, a coupon for carpet cleaning. Nothing interesting in the mail. She pours herself a very short Scotch, one cube of ice, and some water. "The baby will be fine." She takes a long look out the window. It's been a lonely day.

There's a sticky note on the table with her name on it. Curious, she picks it up. Something drops off with a little clink. It's a USB thumb drive. "Weird." She opens her laptop and pushes the USB drive into an open port. A moment later, a video starts to play.

She immediately knows what it is but can't imagine where the video came from. Her memory of this moment is crystal clear; it's something she will never forget.

She and John are sitting on the end of the wooden dock that juts out into Laurel Lake. It's a perfect, late summer day, warm and breezy. Other than a few Canadian geese, they are alone at the lake. John dives in next to her, and the splash makes her laugh. When he surfaces, he is holding something. He treads water in front of her. "Katie." He opens his fist and shows her a small, soaked, velvety box and opens it. "No one could make a life better than this, or a partner better than you." It's his grandmother's engagement ring. "Will you marry me?"

Before she can say yes, the video goes black and stops.

Panic, pain, regret, and longing overtake Katie. She misses him so much. She misses the life they had.

As tears fill her eyes, a memory surfaces. She and John, hand in hand, walking on West 21st Street between 7th and 8th Avenues. Summer, the trees heavy with lush green leaves, birds, and squirrels. In front of them, a chalk-marked hopscotch grid drawn by a young child. He hopped through, counting as he jumped. He played like a kid and lived like a man. He was her other half.

No Good Deed

EACH DAY, Brooke sets priorities and delays orders she deems less important or unimportant. Then, she passes the orders to Mike.

Today's orders are stacked neatly on Mike's desk, next to a cup of black coffee. *It's not hot enough*, he thinks.

The office door bursts open and bangs against the rubber stop on the floor. Katie heads directly for him, her eyes intense and sleepless.

"Hi, morning, a word?!" she snips, firmly taking his arm. "I have something I want to show you."

"Oh, what?"

She directs him out of the office, through the waiting room, and onto the street. The nut vendor is still there.

Katie doesn't say a word as she opens her fist. The USB thumb drive rests on her palm.

"You found it!" he says with pride.

"Where did this come from? There wasn't anyone else there—no cameras, nobody!" The confusion and chaos of trying to understand how this could exist is wrecking her brain.

"We keep records," Mike says nonchalantly. "It helps things run smoothly. Didn't you see some of these at your interview?"

"What, the testimonials?! Those were infomercials, actors...." She watches him shake his head no. "....They were real?"

"Life is documented. All of it."

"Explain."

"People's faults, failings, transgressions; their joy, their agony. Everything."

That means... so was hers.

"So, I could watch my grandfather build that teak dock at the lake house?"

"Yeah."

"I could understand why my parents were the way they were?"

"Right."

She could see the whole catalog of her life with John, and how it all came to be.

"The Universe works in mysterious ways, Katie."

She can't stand still a moment longer. She begins to pace, her mind racing.

She steps uncomfortably close to his face and, in hushed tones, asks, "Me and John—there's more?"

"Many."

"I have to see them." Desperation fills her eyes. "And my parents, and my...."

"They're off-limits."

"How 'off-limits' can they be?!" She holds up the USB drive.

No good deed goes unpunished, Mike thinks. This didn't make Katie feel any better; it just opened the floodgates.

"I thought it would make you feel better. He seemed like a great guy."

"Yeah, he was a great guy. He was my best friend, we had a life together, and then he died! Of course it made me feel better, and now you're telling me there's more—there's the whole story and a whole other story that I probably don't even know."

"You have to live now, Katie. If you go back, you'll be doing that every day, and that means you're not going to be doing something else that needs doing."

"Not helping."

"We've got a plan, and a job, and—"

"Not helping, Mike!"

"Look, I know what happens when the plan gets disturbed—wars, disease, death—and who knows what else." He glances over both shoulders. "I can tell you, with first-hand knowledge, at least a hundred and fifty thousand people have died because a kid wanted to feed some damn ducks. And I just disturbed the *damn plan*!"

She doesn't care.

"There have been mistakes, screw-ups. I've made some of them. We have to try to make up for them—to fix that stuff. Keep your memories," he says. "Look at your photos, your stuff, and don't make me explode everything—okay? It's not worth doing any more damage."

Hopes and Dreams #2
The Unicorn

MIKE STANDS ALONE in a cavernous gymnasium. He's wearing a skin-tight, one-piece gymnastics outfit with long legs and a tank top. He shakes his shoulders, shimmies, and rolls his head in a circle; his neck cracks. His hand reaches into a pouch and grabs some chalk. He rubs his palms together, then claps, sending a dusty puff into the air.

Twenty-five meters of runway stretch before him, ending at the vaulting horse he's about to clear.

After a momentary meditation and a deep exhale, his sprint begins. Arms and legs pump in perfect synchronization, laser-focused like an Olympian. His final strides open up as he reaches the springboard. The small, spring-loaded platform compresses under his weight, then catapults him skyward.

Two hands plant firmly on the horse before he pushes away, twisting and spinning. For a moment, he's weightless, defying gravity. He reaches the apex of his flight, then begins his descent.

On the mat in front of him stands a pure white, majestic unicorn. Its silver eyes and silky mane shimmer in the gymnasium lights. It bows its head slightly as Mike spreads his arms, falling like a skydiver without a parachute.

A millisecond later, he's impaled on the horn of the mighty animal. His guts drip down its shimmering white coat.

Back in New York City, Mike's head rests on his pillow. He's dead asleep—and laughing.

OB/GYN

TODAY'S FOLLOW-UP visit to the OB/GYN was marked as a red-letter day weeks ago—the twenty-week pregnancy visit. Katie arrives early, signs in, and takes her spot in the lobby.

"Katie?" A nurse holding a clipboard pokes her head into the lobby. "We're ready for you."

Down the corridor, posters of plump, pretty babies hang on the walls. The nervous, happy buzz of expectant parents and cheery staff fills the air.

"Can you fill this up for me?" She hands Katie a plastic container. "The bathroom is on your left."

"Sure."

"You can put it in that tray when you're done and then go to Room 3. Just there."

A few minutes later, blood pressure, temperature, pulse, and a few questions. *Feeling tired, any cramping, how's the diet?* And then a blood draw. Katie always has to look away when the needle pierces her vein.

The ultrasound machine silently comes to life. The nurse shakes a bottle of gel. "This might feel a little cold."

"It does."

The cold, smooth metal transducer firmly slides across her abdomen, probing sometimes uncomfortably.

"There it is! Hello, little one," says the nurse with a smile. Katie feels gentle pressure.

"We'll get you some pictures." The nurse moves the transducer, then presses a button on the machine. A thermal paper print rolls out, and the process is repeated.

"The doctor will be in in a few minutes. Congratulations."

But it's more than a few minutes. *Busy day in "babyland,"* Katie imagines.

The nurse comes back in and asks, "Do you think you could give me a little more urine?" So Katie does.

A few minutes later, the doctor and her clipboard enter. After the expected pleasantries, the doctor asks in a sober manner, "How are you feeling? Is anything unusual going on in your everyday life? New hobbies, stress?"

Katie recalls the incredible things she's experienced working for the Universe. She decides that she has no idea how to answer those questions, so she just says, "Nothing unusual."

The doctor goes on to explain, "The baby looks healthy, and most everything seems normal." Katie is relieved.

"But there's one thing, and honestly, I'm not sure what to make of it." Katie sees a look of curious concern on the doctor's face. "The baby is just about the same size it was two months ago."

"Sorry, what?" Katie says as she shifts on the examination table.

"The baby hasn't grown—but otherwise it's perfect."

Katie doesn't know what to say. *Distressed* is the look on her face.

"Listen," says the doctor, "we're going to do a little

blood work. I have some ideas. Let's not add any stress to what is an otherwise perfectly healthy kid. Maybe this one keeps time a little differently than the rest of us," she adds with a smile. "I'm sure everything is going to be just fine."

Katie thinks back to her first meeting in the office with Brooke, the job interview.... *"When we officially sign the contract, time will slow down for you."*

Transatlantic

New York Harbor

THE RMS OCEANIC left England nine days ago. The woman wanted to stay for the celebration of Queen Victoria's Diamond Jubilee, but it was time to go.

When they leave Liverpool, it is barely visible. Rain, fog, and the black of night cover the city. The journey across the Atlantic is endless sea, endless sky, and ferocious storms. The vessel, though huge, is still not perfectly stable in rough seas.

The young man vomits several times and takes a beating for it. "This is not the behavior of a young gentleman," the woman says.

"Yes, Mama."

Approaching New York Harbor, the Statue of Liberty, a recent gift from the French, stands tall, her torch held high, welcoming all.

The woman stands on the deck with the young man.

New York rises in front of them. A pigeon lands on the rail of the ship.

"Pigeonneau," she says with a smile.

The bird flutters away.

"This will be our new home." The early morning sun lights up the city. The fiery autumn colors of the trees are evident even from the great distance of the ship.

"Yes, Mama."

The young man has never seen anything like this. Smokestacks, buildings, dozens of vessels navigating the waterways. America. He had only seen the skyline of the city in photographs and newspapers—a city whose energy reaches out into the harbor, across the world. He had read of this place, the turmoil it endured. He is grateful that he had been taught to read. This is not permitted for most with his coloring.

"When we are in America, you will call me 'Ma'am' or 'Ms. Newton,' not Mama."

"Yes, M... Ma'am. What is Newton, Ma'am?"

"I am your guardian; I am your caretaker. In America, my name is Ms. Newton—Brooke Newton. Do you understand, Michael?"

"Yes, Ma'am."

34 Commerce

From her well-worn horsehide leather chair, an antique from the early twentieth century, Brooke inspects the wall in her study. The paneling itself is barely visible. Articles, notes, and yarn strung back and forth between pins take up every available inch. She huffs a breath onto her dirty glasses and wipes them on her blouse. Upon closer examination, and with clean glasses, she stands to take a closer look at one of the notes. Something is puzzling her. She knows everything does not always go as planned. Timing is a sensitive thing—interpretation, instinct. Sometimes, adjustments need to be made.

She learned this many years ago. Most things that need adjusting take a minor change here or there and can be resolved within days or months. *Most* things.

She pulls a thick, black, leather-bound book from a shelf. *Seems heavier than it used to. I'm getting old*, she thinks. She finds an open spot on the table between stacks of books and papers and opens it. Annotated, colored sticky notes mark pages of interest from beginning to end. Brooke scans a few of the notes, flipping through the pages. *Where is it?* she wonders, running her finger down one page, then another, then a third.

"Ah," she stops on a passage. "Yes." She marks the page, writes a note, and tacks it to the wall. Closing the book, she pulls out a folder and, from it, a yellowed sheet of paper. She reads something on the sheet. "Right." A quick jot onto another sticky note, which she then places on the wall next to the intersection of three strands of yarn.

"Okay," she says. "Better."

A truck rumbles by outside. Her phone rings.

"Hello?"

"I need to see you." It's Katie, and the urgency in her voice is apparent. "Can I come over?"

"Anytime. 34 Commerce Street, downtown," Brooke replies.

"What's the apartment number?"

"Just 34 Commerce. It's a house."

And so it is, though a rarity in Manhattan, a house. A modest brick building tucked away on an ancient street in the West Village. Katie steps out of the yellow cab and ascends the seven steps to the front door. Only a moment after her second knock, she hears Brooke opening the locks.

"I've got the kettle on, come on in." A whistle from a tea kettle beckons. They enter a room at the top of the oak staircase. It's spacious, warm, and loaded with artwork from a myriad of influences.

"I'll be right back."

Katie drifts to an easel by the windows. A painting in progress shows a three-masted sailing ship in stormy seas, flying a Spanish flag. Beautiful technique.

There are paintings of Brooke in period costumes as a younger woman. There is one of her and a young Black man.

"Here you go," Brooke returns with cups of tea. "Chamomile."

"This is you?" Katie asks as she studies the detail of the painting.

"Striking resemblance, isn't it?"

"This looks like Mike."

Brooke joins her at the painting. "It's a hobby of mine I picked up in Paris. What can I do for you, Katie?"

Katie had held back from motherhood for fifteen years. There were other things that, at the time, were higher priorities. There would always be time—they were young, they were in love, and neither was going anywhere. John never forced the issue. Finally, when she was ready to shift gears and take on new responsibilities, he was stolen. But he left something behind.

"I had a doctor's appointment today. My twenty-week appointment at the OB/GYN—I'm pregnant."

An audible gasp escapes Brooke as she covers her mouth. "That is such wonderful news, Katie. Congratulations! Whatever time you need when the baby comes, just let me know."

"About needing time—I'm sure you remember when we met in the office, and we talked about the benefits?"

"Yes, of course."

"I discovered I was pregnant a couple of months ago, and this is pretty much halfway—"

Katie doesn't see the melancholy in Brooke's eyes. *New life coming into the world, it's the greatest thing. I wish I could have contributed in that way*, Brooke thinks.

"—and the doctor told me this morning that the baby is just about the same size as it was in our first appointment."

"But it's healthy, right?"

"Healthy, yes." *How could she know this?* "The benefits

147

we talked about in my interview—you mentioned, 'time slows down,' and...."

"And what did I mean by that?"

Katie pleadingly looks to Brooke, not knowing what to ask, how to deal with the impossible.

Ever since Katie took the job, the impossible kept reshaping itself. The thrill of workdays, with even tiny orders, created a sense of longing during personal time.

She used to look forward to the weekend. Time to do nothing with John, read the paper, catch up on the mail, go see a movie, or get lost in Central Park. A long weekend would mean a trip to Laurel Lake with a sketchpad—imagining a kitchen redesign, considering taking down a wall for a bigger bedroom, fixing a dripping faucet, or fishing off the teak dock. This all seems a lifetime away. All the daily impossible items she deals with involve other people, things, and events. Now, what is arguably the biggest event of her life is caught in this web.

"It's time you know all the details, Katie, because *you* are a key person in all of this."

"Okay," Katie whispers with an exhale.

"I was chosen for this job when I was about twenty-five years old. I was in Italy when I was called. I had just lost my best friend—she died during childbirth. She was practically my sister."

Her own words give her pause. Sadness. "Sister...," she whispers. Her eyes are momentarily a million miles away.

"I want to show you something."

Brooke pulls a thin wooden box with ivory and onyx inlays from one of the shelves. The box had rested dead center of the shelf, seemingly in a place of honor.

A key protrudes from a lock on the box. A metallic *click* as it's turned, the *squeak* of the hinged door as it's opened.

"I found a message from the Universe."

She extracts a faded, ancient sheet of paper from the box. Its edges are cracked, a corner torn away.

"I was called and couldn't say no. The work was so compelling, helping people and making a difference in the world."

Brooke sets it in front of Katie. She only looks, afraid to touch the treasure.

"It took me a long time to recognize the importance of the work. The significance of it. Do you feel like you have made a difference, Katie?"

"Yes," she involuntarily smiles. "It's been amazing at times."

The document is handwritten, and not in a language Katie recognizes. "Can you read that?" she asks.

"Yes—it's a very old German dialect. Something like, 'Embrace the Universe, and the world will change around you.' Rough translation, but that's the idea." Brooke takes Katie's hand. "I embraced it. I was taught what to do and how to do it, how to change the world. And there's so much more you will do, Katie. More to know, more lives to change."

"But the baby, Brooke—the baby."

Katie was twenty-four when she and John first discussed children. "There's plenty of time," she said.

She told him that thirty would be the right time to do it, after having had a chance to establish herself in her career.

Thirty came and went.

"The promotion is important to me, John, and as long as it's before thirty-five, we don't have worries about health." When she turned thirty-six, more discussion came about career, advancements in science, and even bringing up surrogacy. John drew the line there. He didn't want a third party involved.

All their friends became less and less available. They were starting their own families. Katie didn't want those trappings. She wanted independence for her and John. She wanted early retirement and to travel, not diapers and birthday parties.

And now the choice is gone. John is gone, but his child remains, and it's in limbo.

"The baby will come," says Brooke, "and it will be fine—in about seven years."

"Seven years? I can't. I quit."

Brooke can see the tension in Katie's face and body, her clenched fists. "It's just not quite that easy. You will know when you're done, when all of your work has been finished. The baby will come then. It will just happen."

Katie sets down her tea, unblinking. The cup clinks against the saucer.

"People conscripted by the Universe roughly age one year for every ten."

The numbers start churning in Katie's head.

"I have been helping to shape the world for over four hundred years. I wanted to quit myself, more than once." Katie can do nothing but stare. "Something I learned from the people who taught me is that one day, I would have to help the next chosen one to flourish. Katie, you are that person."

"Me? Why me?"

"I only know that the sequence of events which is your life ripples into a future of peace, harmony, and prosperity. I can see possible futures, and most of them, presuming tasks are done and done well, are bright. As bright as you can imagine."

"Most of them?" *Breathe*, Katie tells herself, her chest tightening.

"You completing your tasks, letting your child come into this world, is step one. When the child does come, you must be cautious. There are possible futures in which the important person, who is your child, is in jeopardy."

"How can you know all this?"

"We just know. And knowing you're here makes me feel so much better. I believe in you to protect existence. You'll figure out how to put your puzzle pieces together. One day, you will teach the one who is your replacement—and until then, life as we know it is in your hands."

The breeze through the elm trees on Bleeker Street, an argument in front of a bodega and car horns on 6th Avenue —these make up the late night symphony. "Life as we know it?" she mumbles as she weaves her way through the West Village. "No pressure." *I'm supposed to be growing tomatoes with John and doing some casual consulting*, she thinks. *I didn't sign up for this.*

Who to talk to? Shelby? Too much magic for a civilian. Brooke? It sounds like she's got one foot out the door. Mike —but will he be pissed that he was passed over? What about seniority?

Taking over now sets her up for failure. "Failing is not an option."

She thinks back to the bike messenger. Would the package have been delivered either way? It's impossible to know. The fire in Queens, the Brazilian move, the rain forest find? Massachusetts? Arizona? Peru?

"If I stop something or start it, am I the cause of all the

ripples?" *Did I hurry it up or slow it down? Was it going to happen anyway? How many millions of things happen every day?*

She wishes John was here, but if he was, she wouldn't be anywhere near this mess.

Katie *did* predict that she would take over. She was right, though this was not the path or on the terms that she imagined.

She passes the comedy clubs on MacDougal. Smokers gather outside, performers pantomime in the reflection of car windows. It's a normal night in New York City. Sirens wail in the distance, patrons chatter in restaurants, couples young and old walk hand in hand or arm in arm. There's music playing in Washington Square Park, *probably near the arch*, she thinks. She needs the calm of the green space in the park and stops to sit on one of the benches. A skateboarder silently coasts by.

Can it be worth it?

Katie's stomach is in knots; she can feel a cold sweat on the back of her neck. Brooke's words, a possibly endless commitment, stick in her chest, strangling her.

"What the fuck is this all about?"

Her hands find her midsection. *There's a tiny person in there*, she thinks, *and this can't be good.* She tries to take her mind somewhere, anywhere else.

A place that isn't one that holds the weight of the world, the fate of everyone's existence. Somewhere good.

Barefoot. Walking to the dock her grandfather built. Cattails weaving in a summer breeze. The planks are warm. Summer sun and heavy clouds, humidity and the buzz of insects. She sits—her toes find the cool lake. She lifts one foot out and water drips from her heel. John is out in the rowboat, asleep under a straw hat. Overhead, a seagull floats on the breeze and two sparrows play a game of chase.

Her palms make slow circles, caressing the only connection she can imagine to her past.

What will it look like? What will its laugh sound like? What will it be like to hold this being and feel its breath and its heartbeat as it falls asleep in her arms? What should be done for this *important person* to be happy and safe and whole?

She closes her eyes and pulls shallow breaths, then a little deeper, and deeper still. Her palms find her thighs. She consciously relaxes her fingers. She can feel them spreading and the muscles in her arms and shoulders dropping.

Her heart slows, her breath is full. Slowly, her eyes creep open, staring dead ahead. The sun will rise tomorrow. She knows what she's going to do.

Playing Hooky

BIRDSONG IS in the cool morning air. The sun, still low in the sky, collides with the skyscrapers. Their shadows stretch across the Hudson River.

"Good morning, morning, hi." Katie forces a smile as she checks in at the office. The work orders for the day are laid out. She wants to stay local today. She grabs three and heads out the door. Serious Tier One business on the island of Manhattan.

One by one, she visits the locations of each order.

The first one is uptown: some scaffolding is missing a bolt. Without it, the structure will crash and injure three workers. One of them will miss the rest of the day at work and not stop an assassin on their way to kill a foreign dignitary outside the French Consulate on 5th Avenue.

Katie will find a loose, bent, sixteen-penny nail on the sidewalk and put it in where the bolt should be.

She should be there by 10:15 in the morning, no later, to stop an international incident.

Then on to Battery Park. On one of the ferry boats that

takes tourists to the Statue of Liberty and Ellis Island, a pipe bomb will go off.

The ferry will capsize, and thirteen people will die. One of them is pregnant with twins. One of the twins has something in her genome which will be found to cure Alzheimer's disease.

Katie is going to "accidentally" trip the bomber with the handle of an umbrella. That will delay him enough to miss the boat.

This job is set for 1:20 in the afternoon, hours from now.

Then she'll take the 4 or 5 train from Bowling Green and a quick walk to 59th and Lexington. She has to padlock an entrance at a department store. A kidnapping will be averted.

The victim would be a teenager who, with her upcoming science fair submission, would invent a solar charging device capable of fixing global warming.

"Lock the door at 4:17 p.m.," the order says.

She remembers Mike telling her on her first day, *"If you miss a step or do something out of order, or get the orders out of order, things can get bad."*

Things can *get bad*, she thinks, *not* will *get bad*. Is there some wiggle room?

Mike had promised an explanation of what "bad" meant, but it has yet to be given. *Are we talking about physical repercussions? Fires, explosions, tidal waves?*

In her hands are three sheets of paper, with print on both sides: the summary, the particulars, the timing, and the cone diagram filled with expected outcomes.

John's words from his last day on Earth echo in her head: *"Things find a way to work themselves out, Kate. Let's take a day off and have another look."*

* * *

She looks again at each order, imagining the people who have no idea of the strings being pulled on their behalf.

What a world, she thinks.

She drains the coffee cup, folds the orders in half twice, and shoves them back into the zip pocket of her jumpsuit. It's a two-minute walk to the station at 59th and Lexington.

Katie boards the downtown N to the NYU stop and then takes a four-minute walk to the multiplex cinemas at 830 Broadway. She buys three movie tickets, a large popcorn, and a root beer Icee. She will stay in the theater and not check her phone, or any news of any kind, for the rest of the day.

I will look tomorrow morning, she thinks. *Things find a way to work out.*

Following the movie plots is impossible. What romance, between whom? What superhero? What supervillain? There's not some big sweeping event that makes everything all right, or one person who changes the future. It's a few select worker bees. They make the tiny adjustments that have consequences. The consequences start chain reactions of events that keep everything on track.

Of the three films she watches, the last one is the most enjoyable—a foreign film in German. It's slow and quiet, and if she slides down in her seat, the subtitles are out of view. It's nice to look at the pretty pictures and listen to the mixture of orchestral film score and house music. The dialogue has no meaning.

She makes up the story as it goes along, deciding it's about two people growing old together, raising a wonderful human being, and living in an old house by the lake. At this, she smiles.

On the crosstown walk home, she sees nothing out of the ordinary. Late-night diners. Music and chatter from pubs. The moon playing hide-and-seek behind fast-moving clouds, one of which looks like a dragon. The smells wafting from carts peddling pretzels or hot dogs are tempting, but not enough to make her stop. The pace of her boots sounds out a small-town tempo in the big city.

Later, inside Apartment 4F, Katie lies in bed with her eyes open. Shadows move across the ceiling as late-night cabs pass by. Thoughts of the day that just passed, and the one to come, dance around her head. Peaceful visions of the past and the hitchhiker inside her body comfort her. A calm creeps over her face, and she drifts off. Her dreams are serene and peaceful. It's a beautiful day at Laurel Lake; she's swimming with John and wearing his grandmother's ring.

When the morning light creeps in on Katie's smiling face, her eyes open. She is still in the dream with John. She smiles, stretches, and rolls over. John's side of the bed is empty. He must be making coffee. For a moment, she has forgotten that he is gone, and about her new job and yesterday's experiment. That moment evaporates, and in the next, her laptop is open.

After a few minutes of scanning all the local news sites, she throws on a robe and runs downstairs to the newsstand. *The New York Post* and *The New York Times* are in neat stacks. They don't have any blaring headlines. She looks around at the normal New York City morning: people walking their dogs, making deliveries, taking cabs—life. No chaos.

72nd and Broadway—the uptown Number 1 train clatters into the station. Katie weaves her way to the exit and ascends into Verdi Square, a small patch of walkways, newsstands, and greenery among the Upper West Side chaos.

Up Broadway a half-block, the left lane is coned off. The lights on a Con Edison truck silently blink. A flatbed truck stacked with wood planks and metal tubes has its flashers on, and workers are moving materials. Three NYPD cruisers and six officers congregate. A handcuffed man in the backseat of one of the cruisers shouts through closed windows at no one.

Katie surveys the scene from across the street, her eyes darting from the police to the utility workers.

"What's going on?" a college kid wearing a Wisconsin sweatshirt asks.

"Don't know." She runs across the street, waving a cab past her.

"Officers," she calls to the group. Two of them turn. "What's happening?"

The Nordic-looking, mustached policeman scans Katie, deeming her simply curious. "Loose bolt on some of that scaffolding." He points to workers resetting metal tubes and thick wooden planks. "Nobody hurt, but that guy got trapped." He thumbs to the prisoner in the back of the cruiser. "He was carrying a couple things he shouldn't ought to have. Lucky break for everyone else really," he says.

"Oh my—like a bomb or something?" *Be coy, be charming*, she thinks.

"He had a thirty-eight and a pocket full of zip ties. Sounds like trouble to me," he says with a wink.

"Lucky break indeed," she says. "Thanks, Officer."

Was that the assassin?

* * *

The crosstown 72 bus through the park takes about twenty minutes. She exits at 59th and Lexington.

It's always busy here; shopping never stops. A cluster of people at one corner watches a juggler, and at another corner, a preacher aggressively shares his message.

Two news vans are parked nearby. Reporters are on camera, their tones serious, their skin a little too perfect and taut. Katie gets close enough to hear a young woman say, "I'm a blue belt, and my instincts just took over. I guess that training really works."

"What message do you have for your assailant? For other young women?" a reporter asks.

"For him? I hope he gets the help he needs—or gets ready to face this." She displays a clenched fist. The crowd laughs and hoots. "Girls, you can learn to protect yourself; do it. And don't let the assholes win! Sorry, can I say that?"

She fought back, Katie thinks. *Things take care of themselves.*

* * *

Every four minutes the Number 4 or 5 train stops at the 59th Street station. Once aboard, Katie is seventeen minutes away from Bowling Green and the ferry docks at Battery Park.

The Number 5 train pulls in with a squeal. Katie grabs a side-facing seat. An advertisement in her line of sight features diverse, smiling young faces and promotes LaGuardia Community College with the slogan "Build Your Future." Someone has colored in a few of the teeth of the model students.

The train pulls into Grand Central. Few exit the train, many board. Like cattle being driven into a pen. A hunched, wrinkled old woman clutches a cloth shopping bag in one hand and a chrome pole in the other, hoping for steadiness. Katie catches her eye and waves her over. "Take my seat," she says. The woman smiles and thanks her. *An unscripted good deed.*

Katie emerges from the tunnels a few stops later at Bowling Green. She scans the area, and there's no evidence of anything out of the ordinary. Tourists wait for tickets and queue up to board the next boats to Ellis Island and the Statue of Liberty. No police, nothing roped off. No fire-ravaged ferry boat crawling with investigators. No weeping relatives or small shrines to the dead. She must be discreet.

Katie spots an information booth. A uniformed high school student—tall, lanky, sporting a pimple patch—is behind the counter. "What happened here yesterday?" Katie asks, as though she knew something bad had happened.

"What?" he asks with a curious look.

"I heard about a fire or bomb or something." She's trying to be nonchalant about it. "Were you here yesterday?"

"Oh yeah, I was here."

Talking to teenagers can be annoying; they give such short answers. She looks at the name tag—it's time to take the direct approach.

"Toby, that's your name, right?"

"Yeah!" He's surprised. "How'd you know?"

"Toby, was there a problem here yesterday? Did someone get on a boat with a bomb? Did anyone get killed?"

Toby glances in both directions and leans in to her. "Are you a cop?"

She leans in and lowers her voice. "I'm a detective—Toby, what do you know?"

His eyes sparkle ever so slightly.

"We're not supposed to talk about this, but since you're a cop, uh, detective, I guess I can tell you," he says for his own assurance.

"Yes, please do." She offers a serious nod.

"Okay, so this dude is running for the ferry. He was barely going to make it. He was yelling something like, 'I'm coming! Wait, wait! Blah, blah.' So the ship guy unclips the rope to let him on. The dude is still running, and all of a sudden, he trips over this lady's double stroller, knocks it over. The babies were freaking out. And the guy falls over the ropes into the bay, right?"

"Right."

"So the security guys throw a thing, one of the round things that float, y'know?"

"A life preserver."

"Right, life preserver, and they fished him out. So guess what?"

"What, Toby?"

"The dude had a vest of dynamite or something on. And it all got wet, and didn't explode."

"No kidding."

"The security guys start yelling, the people back off, and the guy gets shoved face down in the grass and handcuffed."

And there it is, Katie thinks, *working itself out.*

"Some cops showed up a few minutes later, and that was that."

She put her hand firmly on Toby's shoulder. "The mayor will send you a medal. It's best if you don't tell anyone else this story, okay?"

He's beaming. "Okay, Detective."

"You're a credit to all New Yorkers, Toby. You should be proud of yourself."

Out of the corner of her eye, she notices she's holding

up the line. A very European-looking couple stands behind her, their stylish, understated clothes and polite patience giving them away. The slender, silver-haired gentleman and the round-faced woman with the long braid nod and smile.

"Good morning," he says with an unmistakable French accent.

"Bonjour," Katie replies, stepping aside.

"Merci," they say.

She smiles. "You're welcome."

Finally, her two years of French in high school have paid off.

This day has been exhausting.

For the first time in a long time, she has something to look forward to when she gets home.

Back in the West Village, in Apartment 4F, the thumb drive Mike had left for her is still mounted in the USB port. She presses play and spends the remainder of her waking moments with John.

* * *

"This is a little awkward," Katie says, handing Mike a coffee, "but I'm going to report you to Brooke if you don't set me up with more of those videos of John. Like a regular delivery."

Mike searches her face for any emotion that matches her request—desperation, anger, or even something darker. But her tone is so matter-of-fact that all he feels is terror. He knows the consequences of breaking the rules: the sinking of the *Titanic*, World War II, and his personal demon, John Wilkes Booth killing Abraham Lincoln.

"The rules...," he pleads.

"But *you* broke the rules. You showed me that recording. It probably doesn't matter if you've done it once or a hundred times. You broke the dam, it's done."

He thinks of Brooke, the long voyages they'd taken to Africa, England, Europe, America. She'd shared her own misadventures—what happened when she took matters into her own hands. The small, benign acts that led to disastrous consequences. She had warned him that even his own life was somehow at risk.

"Why?"
"Because of the destruction you have caused."
"Yes, Ma'am."

He was guilty, too. Peeking behind the curtain. Too curious about how things worked, how the details intertwined. The temptations were too great.

"That's not the first time I broke the rules. And I don't even know what might have happened the other times."

The other times, the curiosity, the conscience. He had heard stories of wonder and horror, but never seen proof.

"But it doesn't make sense, how do we know?"
"Because the tasks are before us and lives are at stake. You must believe."

Katie, we can't decide which rules we're going to follow and which jobs we're going to do. It's too dangerous."

He averts his gaze; he knows the truth of how he feels.

"I don't have any idea if anything that I've done in the last four hundred years matters," he tells Katie.

"What if things just find a way to figure themselves out?"

"What if they don't?!"

Katie takes a defiant breath. Her agenda is unchanged.

"What if they do?"

She slowly recounts every little detail about what *didn't* happen yesterday.

Mike listens. He runs worst-case scenarios in his head. She tells him about the follow-ups: the guy with the gun, trapped under some scaffolding; the girl who knew karate; the bomber who tripped over a double stroller.

He's in a cold sweat.

"What do you want to do?"

The Archives

It's the twenty-second day of the month. The office is closed. Katie and Mike meet outside the building at 8 a.m. The nut vendor isn't there.

Inside, the morning sun reflects off the "Out of Service" elevator door.

"We call it the 'Archives,'" Mike says as he inserts a key into the padlock. "If you ever come in here, be sure to count the links on the chain that hang past the lock. It has to be locked up the way you found it. See here, one link on this side, five on this. She changes it every few days. Do you understand?"

"Check."

"To open the door, press the 'up' button three times." And he does. The door slides open with a creak.

The inside of the elevator is common. It looks like any other pass-through elevator with an additional set of doors on the back side. The buttons for selecting the floor are unusual, though. They count from zero to nine.

"The code for opening the back door is 1-1-3-4-0-4-5-2-4-6-4, then the 'down' button," he says as he presses the sequence. Katie pats her pockets for a pen, but before she finds one, the doors slide open.

"I'll write that down for you. Once the back doors open, you can find a light switch around the corner."

"This room is huge." Her eyes follow the blinking dots of light that recede a seemingly endless distance. "Do we have the building next door?"

"Think Frosted Glass Door," he says. "We're somewhere in Eastern Canada."

A table, about the size of a long dinner table for twelve, stands in front of them. At one end, there's a water dispenser with paper cups, and at the other, a stack of papers that look like orders. In the center of the table sits an old-style computer monitor, with a keyboard and mouse beside it. The mouse rests on an "I Love New York" mousepad.

"All this," he says, gesturing to the shelving lined with ever-blinking lights, "is controlled by that computer." He moves the mouse, positioning the cursor over a field on the screen, then taps a key on the keyboard. "And this," he continues, "is how we start the review process."

"Review?"

"Events, happenings, the world at work."

The look on Katie's face says she doesn't understand.

"Think of it like a historical research tool. If we need to find something to help us keep things up and running in the Universe, we can look here."

"Like the internet?"

"But better. Press it." He indicates the *VIEW* button. She looks to him and raises an eyebrow, silently asking permission. He nods; permission granted.

She clicks the button, and a twenty-foot-high rectangular hologram showing static appears.

"It displays whatever you search for. Right now,

because we haven't searched for anything yet, it's blank. It's essentially a movie screen."

He pulls out the chair tucked under the table. "You drive."

Katie sits and raises the chair a little bit to get comfortable. She repositions the ancient keyboard and mouse. The query form on the screen waits for input.

"Here," he points, "you can type in information to these fields when you're looking for people and events. Some fields have preset values and drop-down menus. For example, you could do an external search for civilians or an internal search for employees. You can also use the microphone. Click the field you want, hold down this button, and talk. There's an art to asking the right questions; if it's not phrased correctly, you might not get the answer you're looking for. I usually just type it in."

"How do I get to John?" she asks.

"Let's start broad, and then drill down. Start with first and last name."

She enters, *JONATHAN PAULSON* in the *NAME* field.

"Then 'Enter.'" She taps the button.

A massive batch of search results return. A list shows on the screen. Katie had no idea there were so many John Paulsons in the world.

"Okay, now we get more specific."

He walks her through a few parameters to narrow the results: year of birth, place of residence, year of death, nickname in high school.

Finally, there is one person in the search results. Katie's eyes mist. She looks at Mike. "We found him."

"Click the name."

The moment seems in slow motion. Katie's hand trembles as she looks at his name and the blinking cursor. She pulls away from the mouse, closes her eyes, and takes a deep breath. Mike puts a hand on her shoulder. "Sometimes, it's too hard to look," he says. "I know how you're feeling right now. I've sat in almost the exact same spot."

Her hand hovers back to the mouse.

"You're gonna need some time with this." Mike stands to leave. "I'll be at my desk."

She pulls the mouse across the heart in the middle of the "I Love New York" mousepad, closes her eyes, and clicks.

Finding John

IN FRONT of Katie on the small screen is a long list of moments from John's life: his teenage years, the day they met, their first date, meeting friends and relatives, falling in love, family fractures, and future plans.

Where on earth to start? John shared a lot with Katie, and yet there were things here she had never heard about. "The man had a life before me," she says.

One entry catches her eye. "Oh yes." A small puff of laughter involuntarily escapes her lips. She presses play. The hologram starts to move.

It's John, probably eighteen years old, and Rachel. His first girlfriend. Katie had teased him into showing her Rachel's picture.

"That hair!" she had said at the time.

"Mine was just as bad," was his answer.

Katie had heard the story of this day, but to see it like this gives her some satisfaction. *"I don't know how to explain this, and I'm sorry,"* said John. *"I'm not in love with you. I don't think I'm ever going to be."*

"That's right," Katie says, smiling. "Definitely not his type."

It's like looking through the greatest family photo album ever made.

She goes further back in time. John is twelve, crying and choking on his words. A man lifts a dead dog out of the trunk of a cream-colored Chevy Camaro. *"It just ran out into the street, I'm so sorry."*

Katie remembered this story, too. Patches was a mix of a springer spaniel and a beagle. The dog was running alongside John as he rode his bike from the corner store. It ran into the street to chase a bird and right into the path of an oncoming car. John had described the *yelp!* of the dog to her before, and the terrifying sound of its bones breaking as it tumbled under the car, and the skid of the Camaro. He held back tears anytime he recalled the story or saw a dog that looked similar.

Some moments she remembers perfectly. Some have slipped into her subconscious; others are surprises. His future plans, their plans. How would those plans have played out? She wonders, *what might have happened if he hadn't died? Was he supposed to die?* Katie thinks about that idea in any moment she is alone in the city, or in their bed, or in their kitchen—basically all the time.

This is the biggest emotional rollercoaster she has ever been on. Events spread out over decades, compressed into a single sitting. It's exhilarating. It's exhausting. She needs a break—the water cooler beckons. Bubbles gurgle to the top of the bottle as she fills a paper cup.

"There's an art to asking the right questions," Mike had said.

Looking for John was the plan. The cursor stands,

pulsing slowly on the screen, awaiting command. The hologram stands by.

Katie is, however, mentally full—as after a holiday dinner. Everything looks delicious, everything tastes delicious, and with a gluttonous exhale, the moment arrives when nothing more can be ingested, and the button on your pants must be undone.

The field next to the cursor is filled with the word EXTERNAL and a downward-pointing arrow. As Mike had explained, this indicates that the search is outside of company employees.

Again, like at a holiday dinner when you somehow find room for pie and coffee—and then sneak a second piece of pie right out of the tin—Katie clicks the dropdown menu and changes the query to INTERNAL. She has no idea how long she has been alone in the Archives, watching and searching. She glances over her shoulder, hesitant about her next move, to ensure no one is spying.

Satisfied she's alone, she enters a name on the keyboard, MICHAEL ROMANO, and presses ENTER. A whir of activity emits from the endless stacks of blinking lights. They flicker at a new pace, accelerating. On the screen a list builds rapidly and tumbles past the boundaries of the screen.

It begins with current activity. She recognizes some of their conversations and chats with other coworkers.

"Stay in the game. This is Tier One. Are you ready?" It seems like it's in reverse order of occurrence.

"I told him there was a spider on his face."

"Sometimes you just gotta let off some steam."

The images in the hologram span recent history, near past, then decades, then centuries. Mike's age slowly changing, the world he was in devolving into historical fossils—the 1900s, 1800s, 1700s, and earlier.

The numbers in the lower corner of the hologram keep counting down. *The year*, she guesses. The whirring stops, the lights calm. The cursor blinks at Entry Number 1 in Mike's list. The number on the hologram is 1609. Katie pushes away from the table and stands up. "More than four hundred years ago, he wasn't kidding." Hearing stories from Mike had felt like tall tales—exaggerations spun for entertainment. But now, here it is—his life.

The cursor pulses patiently. The pinpoint lights are relaxed, awaiting instructions. She presses play. The footage is from an awkward angle, in motion. Someone is running. The pinpoint lights flicker and flash. She can't see Mike, but she hears the scuffling of feet—soft shoes on a dirt surface. Mike is somewhere in this; it's his search result. A stressed voice whispers in German. The voice belongs to a young woman. She's carrying a baby. She slips and nearly falls, and the baby starts to cry. Katie gasps as the woman briefly passes through a sliver of moonlight. She slams her fingers on the spacebar to stop the playback, then reverses it frame by frame to get another look. Katie pauses as the woman's face fully enters the light. Her hands clutch the child, her gaze filled with trepidation as she looks over her shoulder— possibly at a pursuer. Katie leans in closer. The shape of the mouth, the high cheekbones, the fiery, intense eyes. There's no mistaking it. "Oh—" Katie whispers. "Brooke."

* * *

Katie is back at the water cooler, wishing she had something stronger. She looks again at the frozen frame, studying the face that she has come to know so well. The one who brought her back into the land of the living.

Katie returns to the keyboard.

Staying on the INTERNAL search, she types the letters, BR. Brooke's name immediately populates the search field. *Should I be doing this?* Katie wonders. She thinks about what she had told Mike: *"It probably doesn't matter if you've done it once or a hundred times."* She's definitely over the limit. Her index finger taps the ENTER key.

Lights flash, the Archives whir; the screen fills with records as they compile. Their meeting at the diner over rhubarb pie: *"I believe things happen for a reason, Katie.... The Universe has a plan."* After her stop at the bookshop: *"The nest! I donated those...."* Decades before preaching the gospel of the Universe: *"You think the world can take care of itself? You must have faith."*

On a winter day, Brooke walks across a country road. Her fashion looks like it's from a couple of decades ago. She unties a rope on the back of a stake-bed truck with Canadian license plates hauling caged animals.

Then, with Mike as a younger man, as a boy. Desert and camels, the Eiffel Tower under construction, aboard a ship in an endless ocean. What had Brooke said? *"A bunch of globally-connected, forward-thinking do-gooders who make a difference in almost everyone's life on the planet."*

Same as Katie's experience. After the initial shock and thrill of the job, it just turns into a job. *Even mundane*, Katie thinks—until she sees something that chills her to the bone.

Brooke is young, maybe twenty, and she's holding a child. Her foot presses on a woman's neck, suffocating her. Brooke hisses at her in German.

Whatever Brooke is saying, her feelings about the woman are clear when she spits in her face. Katie gasps as Brooke shifts her weight, forcing all her strength onto the woman's throat.

The woman's larynx collapses under the pressure. She chokes, gasps, and twitches into death.

Brooke is now running with the child through an ancient city. Katie sees what looks like the Vatican. Brooke is speaking in German, her tone sweet and calming as she tries to soothe the crying child. And shockingly, Katie understands two words.

Michael Romano.

Brooke strangled that woman and stole her baby.

Katie slams her hand down and stops the playback. Her eyes dart around the room to ensure there's no one else there. "She killed his mother and took him," Katie whispers under her breath. "Now—what the fuck is this all about?"

With those words, a mechanical sigh is followed by an acceleration of clicking and whirring from the Archives. The frozen image on the hologram disappears with a flash, and the entire display turns black. The room starts to buzz, the computer screen rapidly compiling something. Every machine in the warehouse clicks and whirs. "What did I do?" Katie sees her hand on the button that opens the microphone. Videos start to play frantically—major world events and history raging around her: war, peace, love. Mike saves someone, then saves someone else. He has been involved in shaping modern history. She jets back through time—the building of civilizations, Africa, Asia, Europe, early man, dinosaurs, prehistoric times, Pangea. Earth forms its crust, star fields, open space, suns exploding, planets forming, darkness, and then the monumental explosion of the Big Bang.

Katie has to shield her eyes; the intensity of the light is unbearable. Everything is white, and she is temporarily blinded and breathless. There is no sound, only the emptiness of an absence of oxygen. Katie can hear her own heart-

175

beat. She's alone, standing in a massive white nothingness. Every direction she looks is empty white space—except for one point. Her eyes settle on something and she's drawn to it: a message. She gasps, laughs, and then—involuntarily—tears and a gasp of laughter and joy.

Katie closes her eyes, drawing deep breaths to calm herself. When she opens them, the endless white space is gone. She's back in the Archives, standing at the table in front of the old computer.

The cursor blinks next to the words, WHAT THE FUCK IS THIS ALL ABOUT?

* * *

The clock on the wall in the office reads just after midnight. Katie had been in the Archives for about sixteen hours.

Her head is buzzing from what she had seen. She has a million questions, and a million things to share.

The city is ticking outside. The office is empty. She hits the streets.

Somewhere, on another computer screen, a cursor blinks.

Coffee & Bagels

HEAVENLY SMELLS waft from a corner breakfast restaurant on Avenue A.

"Did you find everything you were looking for?" Mike asks as he dunks a bit of bagel in his coffee.

"And more."

They sit in a booth by the window. The morning crowd is fueling up for the day.

"You okay?"

How do I even begin? Katie thinks. What she had absorbed inside the Archives was thrilling, devastating, revelatory. It had turned her world upside down.

A slender, silver-haired waiter stops at their table with a coffee pot. "Hello again! More coffee for you two?" he asks with a French accent.

Katie recognizes him from the information booth at Battery Park. "Well, hello. Small world." She puts a hand over her cup. "None for me, thanks."

"Definitely." Mike pushes his cup toward the edge of the table; the waiter tops off his coffee.

"Bonjour," he says with a wink as he departs.

There's something about his face that Katie finds reassuring—grandfatherly. She thought the same thing at Battery Park. Some people are just like that; they exude calm, comfort, and trust. It's how she feels about Mike.

"What do you remember about your mother, Mike?"

"My mother? Nothing. Why?"

"Just curious."

"She died when I was born. Brooke actually knew her. I guess they grew up together."

"Friends?"

"Yeah."

"When I was in there, I looked you up."

"I figured you would. I did the same thing when Brooke told me John Wilkes Booth was my fault. I must've spent a week trying to get to the bottom of it—poor Abe Lincoln. I probably didn't ask the right questions."

Was it even true? Katie wonders.

"You must have found out that my mom was a slave. After she died from typhus, Brooke tried to *mother* me the best she could."

Tried to mother the best she could. Katie rolls that around in her mind for a minute. Brooke killed a slave girl and stole her baby. Then conscripted him into doing her bidding for four hundred years.

"I'm sure she did," she lies.

Mike has lived in the dark since 1609. How do you tell someone they've been lied to since before the Pilgrims set foot on the North American continent? How could Brooke carry such a guilty secret for so long? Maybe after the first hundred years, you become numb to it.

How do you crush a friend by revealing that the people they trust the most have never once told them the truth?

"Did you look yourself up?" he asks.

"No."

She hadn't thought of that.

"I guess you should know—since we're talking about truth and stuff, I looked you up." He licks a bit of cream cheese off his pinky finger. "You've got an interesting story."

"Anything to be embarrassed about?"

"You didn't kill a president, or sink a ship, or start a war or two."

"That's a relief."

"From what I've seen, it could be much worse."

She chuckles at his impossibly far-fetched statement. What could be worse than starting a war? Pestilence, widespread famine, pandemic, erasing existence?

"You know how Brooke is always studying and connecting dots, deciding what things mean?" Mike asks.

"That's what she does in her office all day. I've seen it."

"All day, all night. Putting together the puzzle. She has her hands on everything that needs to be nudged, influenced, and adjusted. The woman is obsessed."

Katie remembers the book Brooke gave her on day one. "Puzzle pieces," she whispers.

The hand-bound book that contains everything that was nudged, influenced, and adjusted in the lead-up to Katie meeting Brooke.

"She told me I'm supposed to take over. That she's done—"

"Done?"

"—and if we do everything right, we'll be on the right path. The future is—what did she say?—*as bright as you can imagine*. And that we have to protect my kid, if it ever comes, because they're an important person," she says.

"I know I'm not prepared for all this. I mean, I have the book she made for me, which makes zero sense. I have the time on the job, and the time with you, but I'm not even *middle management*." Katie needs to move. She shifts in the booth. "If it should be anyone, it should be you."

The goals that once seemed so important—gardening, tossing stale popcorn to ducks, finding the best tomatoes— now feel like they're a galaxy away. She's stepped away from her usual path: getting really good at something that pays well and that she can tolerate. There are no stakes in selecting a color palette or choosing a font, creating a pretty and efficient layout for a sales piece.

That was the life she once occupied. Blissfully ignorant of the behind-the-scenes work that now consumes her days and haunts her dreams. Any moments of quiet are filled with a desperate yearning for her past, for John. Even though she can plug in and find him, he's just a ghost.

"I can't do it, Mike. I can't run the show."

"She said she wants you to run the show?"

"Yes!"

"You're not ready."

"I know!"

"And that's not what you're meant to do anyway."

"What do you mean?"

* * *

Brooke had told Mike the stories of others like them. She revealed that they were not alone in helping shape the world with actions both large and small. After they left France for Rotterdam following Napoleon's defeat, Brooke became obsessed with correcting her mistakes and negligence. She became fixated on protecting the boy and herself, piecing together clues about their future by burning the corners of their orders.

"Remove the black-inked square and the blue circle from an order and burn it. The next order in the sequence of events will be delivered," the couple who visited them in Paris had instructed.

And so she did. She needed the boy—her son, Mike—to share in this quest. After all, his life was at stake too, wasn't it? Brooke discovered, through careful study, that even in the adjustments they were making to everyday life, there was room for improvement. Even when a job was done wrong, mistakes were not always a bad thing. The *Titanic* and The Beatles—fifteen hundred lives and more than a million pounds sterling in exchange for timeless music for generations.

Brooke delved into history, the Bible, books on the occult, the Eastern cultures. They all share certain traits: a martyr, a prophet, a doomsayer, a hero, and a simpleton who makes a difference.

This last role is theirs. *But not our* only *role*, she thinks. The prophet; she can see the paths. She shows them to Mike and teaches him what they mean. She could be a hero, by saving the boy and herself so they could continue their work. She could rebuff the doomsayers by making small adjustments of her own, and seeing the results, good or bad, which she could run with, or run from.

But then, a problem. A wall. An *insurmountable* wall.

All the orders, all the futures, lead to a place she fears: her own end at the hand of an inferior, and the boy, alone in the world. How could he protect himself?

Her only choice is to strike first—slowly, methodically, across generations. She will wait for the right moment: find the locksmith and the housekeeper, arrange an "accident" that will also result in their deaths. She will facilitate the introduction of their daughter to her future husband, then dispose of him and indoctrinate her. Through all of this, she will wield the power of the Universe to snare and tame her only true threat: the unborn child of Katie Paulson.

* * *

Katie toys with the bagel in front of her. "What is it I'm supposed to do?"

"She thinks that *your job...* is to break the Universe."

The Book

KATIE RUSHES up the stairs to her apartment, ignoring a chatty neighbor on the way. Once inside, she brushes aside a short stack of mail that has piled up on top of the book Brooke had given her. Written in graceful calligraphy on the cover are the initials, "K.P."

The book contains *all the clues and hints and secrets.* Hundreds of pages spanning hundreds of years, but without any coherent narrative or explanation. It's like a scrapbook made by a second grader—filled with seemingly random text, diagrams, handwritten notes, and photocopies of old parchments in languages she doesn't recognize.

On the bright side, it seems to be organized chronologically.

1651: Thomasine Osborne, scientist invitation failure.

Who on earth is Thomasine Osborne? And what could that possibly mean?

1861: James Bell, Titanic. Death prevented person of importance from arriving in America.

Who? Why? She flips back to the beginning. 1654: a drawing of a sailing ship. Three tall masts, billowing sails, and stormy seas. *It looks just like the painting Brooke is working on.* In pen beneath the drawing are the words,

Spanish captured Fort Rocher from pirates on Tortuga.

Then, another note:

7 gen. pre-K.P.

What does that mean? Seventh generation before K.P., Katherine Paulson?

Forward again. The 1960s. Three protests against the Vietnam War in San Francisco. Katie recalls her grandfather was there.

The early 2000s. A torn quarter-page of lined paper with an address for a restaurant in Quebec scrawled on it.

Brooke had said, *"This is everything that brought us together. Everything which was nudged, influenced, and adjusted over my time here at the Universe."*

Her time? "That can't be right!"

"It probably is." Mike stands in Katie's open apartment door.

"It's impossible."

"She thinks a believer is less of a threat."

"How am *I* a threat?"

"I wish I knew, but it doesn't work that way."

Like the kid who's going to find the herb in the Amazon, Katie thinks back to one of her first days on the job.

"You're not meant to be part of this. You're supposed to be doing something that might stop everything we do here."

She wonders how one person could be responsible for so much. Then she thinks of Gandhi, Rosa Parks, and Alexander Fleming. Hitler, Charles Manson, Susan B. Anthony, and Abraham Lincoln, who helped free the slaves.

The scrapbook in front of her suddenly seems less consequential. Her personal problems and existential fears, as monumental as they are, fade to black.

She closes the book, and with damp eyes, looks to her friend.

"What?" he asks.

It only takes a few minutes to tell him everything she has learned from her hours in the Archives—Brooke's guilt, his mother's murder, and how he had been ripped from her arms and a life of slavery, only to become a slave to the Universe.

His entire existence—a lie.

Remain Humble

1913
New York

THE ALREADY-MAJESTIC CITY of New York is evolving. Buildings are getting taller. Automobiles are now putt-putting up the avenues alongside the horses, carriages, and streetcars.

"We are in a time of peril—war is coming," Brooke tells Mike as they walk up Broadway past the shops. "We must remain vigilant; we must remain humble."

"Yes, Ma'am. Can we fix things?"

"We must. We could have used Mr. Lincoln's influence with this current group."

"I'm sorry."

Guilt is a heavy burden; Mike understands. She constantly reminds him of his failings and the need to correct the mistakes of past centuries.

"I understand," she says. "I have my own burden. Trying to fix things now makes it less painful to carry. This is what gives me hope—that I can right enough wrongs to earn forgiveness."

"From whom?" he asks.

They continue to walk uptown—past a green grocer and a bakery, a tailor's shop and a watchmaker. His question remains unanswered.

"We need to make a change," she says. "The Universe has told me that you should have your own space. You're a man now. You need to shape your own life."

"Without you?"

Mike had never known life without Brooke as his care-taker, guardian, and moral compass. She raised him, taught him to read and write, how to dress and behave. She warned him about the harsh reality of his skin color. *"We are all the same beneath our skin," she had told him, "but some people will see you as different, bad, dangerous."*

"They don't know me. How can they think that?"

"This is one reason why we must continue our work. These ideas are poison. There are different kinds of people, minds, and beliefs."

"Yes, Ma'am." He had heard this speech many times before.

"We will succeed. We must believe that."

"Yes, Ma'am."

"You must stay humble. You must continue with our work—do you wish to keep on with the work?"

What else would he do? He has never known anything else. Brooke is the boss, the mother, the father, the guide. "Of course, Ma'am."

"I have a place for you that the Universe has provided. A place to start building your life."

* * *

In the early 1900s, the office for the Universe is not yet at its future location in Queens. It is in Manhattan, south of the Brooklyn Bridge near Fulton Market—a small, three-hundred-square-foot, two-room office on Fletcher Street, above an architect's studio. There are two doors at the time which they use for travel, neither made of frosted glass. Only Brooke knows how they work, but it is time to share this with Mike. "One day your responsibilities will grow," she tells him.

Brooke carries the heavy brass rings of skeleton keys that fit the two doors. Each door has three keyholes. A key, or combination of keys, in one or more of the holes, determines the destination.

"Key Number 12 in the middle hole," she tells him, "and Key Number 65 in the bottom hole. This will be your address. Try it."

She gives him the keys—they're heavy in his hand. Each key is etched with a number, and there are fifty keys on each of the three rings.

"Does it matter which goes in first?" he asks.

"Yes, the bottom first. Always the bottom first."

He takes the second ring, with keys numbered fifty-one to one hundred, and pushes Key 65 into the bottom hole. "Turn it?"

She nods. He turns Key Number 65, and it clicks. On the first ring, he finds Key Number 12, inserts it into the middle lock, and turns. Mike's heart quickens at the thrill of uncharted territory. What does it look like? If it's *his* space, does that mean he can keep it as he pleases? Come and go whenever he wants? He looks at Brooke, nervous excitement in his eyes.

"These kinds of doors are very special. They can take us anywhere we need to work or live. They can help us hide in the background. They make it possible to gently touch lives, direct actions, and quite literally, Michael, make the world go 'round."

This idea is thrilling to him. His contained smile is belied by his flushing cheeks.

"There is another door behind this one; that is your new home. Go ahead."

He pulls the first door and they step through. "Pause," she says. "Let the first door close." Mike can hear his own heart beating and the gentle creak of the hinges on the door. The door clicks closed. At that moment, he hears the sounds of steamships, the clicking of streetcars, and the squawking of seagulls.

His eyes seek permission to proceed.

"Go ahead."

His fingers grasp the cool brass doorknob, and with a quarter turn, he opens the second door. He cautiously steps into the room. A Persian carpet graces the center of the wooden floor; he remembers the carpet from Istanbul. An icebox, a stove, a bed, a table, and a chair fill the rest of the space. Two of the walls are papered with a pattern he remembers from Paris. The East River, spanned by the recently-finished Manhattan Bridge, is visible from the windows. Commerce in the form of ships, barges, and delivery wagons is alive outside.

"I will always be near if you need me, and I will miss you terribly, but this is what we must do."

A photograph of him and Brooke hangs on the wall, next to one of Abraham Lincoln and another of the *Titanic*.

"Yes, Ma'am."

Her eyes are moist, her cheeks flush. She touches his cheek and then takes his hands.

"Food and supplies will be sent here for you. The Universe provides."

She turns to go and offers him a comforting smile. Then, at the sound of the door closing, he's alone with the sounds of the river and the city. He's filled with hope, energy, and a new sense of freedom to make his presence felt in the world and play a bigger role in weaving the fabric of the Universe. He sits at *his* table, in *his* chair, and gazes out of *his* windows at the world, and cries.

Padlock

"Now!" Mike insists. They stand outside the elevator on the third floor of the building in Queens, ten feet away from the door to the office of the Universe.

"There are people here!" Katie says. "Let's come back after hours."

"I hooked you up with John. It's your turn."

And there it is. The everlasting rule of tit for tat, quid pro quo, you scratch my back, I'll scratch yours.

"Okay, okay!" she says.

They push through the door into the office and drift casually toward the entrance to the Archives. Brooke's door is closed. The two other people in the office are busy with paperwork.

"You go in and open the back door. I'll stand guard," she says.

Mike gives her an affirming nod. She pretends to look at the day's orders, set out in their usual spot.

Mike is suddenly in her ear. There are now two padlocks securing the chain.

"Did you lock it when you left?" Her look says she

191

didn't. "I told you—count the links—put everything back how you found it."

"I was too busy freaking out, okay!?" she says in a shouted whisper.

"You know what? It doesn't matter. I'm going in. It's time to put it all out there," Mike says. "I'm going to knock those things off." A chrome fire extinguisher hangs on the wall. Mike yanks it off and starts banging on one of the two locks. "I go from being a slave," *bang!* "to being a goddamn slave to this!" *Bang!* "I can't take a piss without it being someone else's idea!"

"You don't know that!" She tries to calm him down.

BANG! The first lock snaps open.

"How about I step in front of an uptown express? Am I

even allowed to kill myself? Or will someone swoop in and do something to save me?"

From across the room comes a calm, even voice. "Yes, Michael, someone would swoop in and save you." Brooke is standing in her doorway with a stack of orders. "I saved you because you were meant for this. You were meant to live."

"I should have been dead centuries ago. You killed my mother."

"And stole him!" Katie chimes in.

"I wanted a baby. I couldn't have my own—your mother was mine, and that made you my property."

"Times have changed," he says with fire in his eyes.

She reaches for his hand. "You have had a remarkable existence thanks to me, Michael."

"My wonderful existence is filled with beautiful dreams about different ways to kill myself, and that's exactly what I'm going to do! It'll be a dream come true." He heads for the door.

"Michael, we don't know *why* we're here. We just know we have to be the guides—or the world will destroy itself." The door strains on its hinges as he blasts through it.

"Katie, we should talk about the Archives. Tell me what you found."

"Did you hear him?!" Katie points toward the door.

"He'll be fine; this isn't his first dramatic performance."

"What is *wrong* with you?!" Katie is on the move.

"The world can't take care of itself, Katie!" Brooke chases after her. "There are guides and writings to study. You need to talk to headquarters and get more experience on the job! The Archives can mislead, and the danger of simply making one's own way can lead down a road to destruction."

"I've seen this sermon, Brooke." Right before she witnessed the murder in the Archives.

"It gives us these," Brooke shoves a few orders into Katie's hands. "For everyone's sake, I have to keep you on the path. You're the one who can save existence or destroy it!" The belief in Brooke's eyes is pure and unwavering, and so is the terror. "Please, listen to me!"

Katie looks at the stack of orders in her hand. The second one is about saving someone's life. The timeframe is *now*—it's Mike.

"I'm going to save him." Katie's determination surpasses Brooke's belief; she pushes open the office door.

"He's not important, Katie; you are! And John had to die so I could show you why!"

Katie slows to a stop.

"It took decades to get you two together. He was your soulmate, and your reaction to his death was predictable."

Katies eyes glisten and squeeze closed; a single tear rolls down her cheek.

"You went looking for everything you had lost—hopes, dreams, family, love—and then came right here, where you belong. I figured out all the details. Most of it's there in the Archives. The clues to why and the answers you're looking for, the understanding of the importance of it, and how I discerned it. Why it had to be done. Don't you see?"

Katie sees the cold, hard earth in the Calvary Cemetery. She remembers helping lower her husband into the hole in the ground. The visits she made just to be near him and what's left of him, slowly absorbing into the earth. She can't go back. John is dead. He's gone. He can't return.

"I do see. They were the puzzle pieces you put together to shape the future. Not for the grand plan or the greater good. It was a murderer's guess."

Subway Station

Every condemned prisoner gets a last meal. Outside the Court Square subway station, Mike picks up a slice of pepperoni pizza and a Coke. Then he grabs a Twinkie from the newsstand. He has always enjoyed the sweet and savory combination. He looks at the city around him: a young mother pushes a stroller with a toddler in tow. Three teenagers huddle in the doorway of a closed business, smoking cigarettes and trying to look cool. *They'll figure it out eventually,* he thinks. *Their parents likely smoke, and they just picked it up. Probably not even a Tier-Two concern.*

Mike shakes that off; he is done thinking about fixing all the problems of the world. He wants to tell the young mother, *"Love your kids and tell them all the truth they can handle, even if you're not quite sure if it's the right thing to do."* He sees how caring she is with the baby and patient with the toddler. There will be other days when things are harder, but that's okay.

Mike stands, looking down the stairs into the subway station. He feels a gentle rush of warm air from an incoming train.

Final Contradiction

KATIE HAD SEEN the beginning of the Universe. "The WHOLE THING is a contradiction!" Her yell echoes up the stairwell as Brooke chases after her. "Life is going to happen, things are going to screw up, people are going to die, no matter what."

One after the other they push through the door onto the sidewalk. The nut vendor is still there.

"We can change things, we HAVE TO change things!" Brooke catches up and grabs her by the shoulders. "Imagine the world if we can fix all this. Imagine how much worse things will be if we don't! We can't give up!"

"Right now, I can save ONE life, and that's what I'm going to do." With that, Katie rips herself free from Brooke's grasp. She sprints across the street and is on the run.

It's all happening—everything Brooke has tried to undo. The decades of research and planning have come to this. Mike told her she was manipulating the plan, but he didn't understand either! Why can't they see?

She desperately chases Katie into the street but will never catch her youth and her Pumas.

"Katie, I DON'T WANT TO DIE!" she screams as she limps across Northern Boulevard. But Katie is out of earshot, and even if she could hear Brooke's pleas, she has a job to do—an order to fill.

Brooke's fists are clenched, her chest knotted, her mind racing with fear. Clouds of emotion and dread are stoking her terror. Everything she has engineered is unraveling. She did the best she could to raise the boy, to help as much as she could, to make a difference. Why is this being allowed to happen? Is this the realization and inevitable result of centuries of calculated maneuvers?

Yes.

"No," she gasps.

A truck swerves to avoid Brooke, its horn blaring. She freezes in terror. The truck narrowly misses a cab, which slams on its brakes, skids on the wet pavement, and spins out of control, crashing into a light pole. The impact of the crash tears loose an electrical wire with a snap and a spark. The loose wire whips toward the earth and touches down into a puddle that Brooke is standing in. With a deafening *crack* and a blinding flash, it electrocutes her.

911 is on the way.

M Train Coming

MIKE SLIDES his MetroCard back into his wallet. He clears the turnstile and steps onto the outbound platform. A woman wrapped in a tattered green blanket sits on the floor. She looks to be in her thirties, fair-skinned, her brown eyes not yet desperate, still holding hope despite a hard year. *She looks hungry*, he thinks.

"I'm not going to need this anymore," he says as he offers her his wallet. Accustomed to handouts, she reflexively extends her hand and takes the brown leather fold.

"Bless you," she says as he walks away and down the stairs to access the platform for the Manhattan-bound M train. She wonders why he put it that way. His head disappears from her view.

Katie is running—she tries to look at the details of the order and avoid tripping on the cracks in the weathered concrete. "Which platform?" she mutters to herself, out of breath. It will be either the E, M, or 7 train. At that moment, she is grateful for the wonders of the Universe, still amazed that they are possible, and still convinced that it doesn't really matter in the grand scheme of things.

But this is not about the grand scheme; it's about Mike Romano. Ripped from his mother's arms. Saved from a life of slavery and conscripted into another kind of slavery for four hundred years. Despite all that, he is a kind, good man who deserves to know that he is valued.

The red LED sign noting the arrival of the next M train reads *"1 minute."* Mike stands on the platform near the back end of the train. He listens for the clicking sounds, one of the first signs of an approaching train. Nothing yet.

It's going to be at nearly full speed at that point and do the most damage, he thinks. He can feel the air shifting. There are only four other people waiting on the platform and no one is too close to him. Mike decides to wait a few moments before jumping onto the tracks.

He finishes his pizza and tosses the last bit of crust down to the third rail. A rat running along the tracks scavenges the crust and nibbles at it. Mike is glad it's going to good use. He takes a deep breath. He can hear the clicking on the tracks, the wind out of the tunnel shifting slightly. The first glimpse of the illumination from the headlight on the M train bounces off the black tunnel walls and down the steel rails. It's time.

Katie emerges onto the platform at the far end. She scans past the others and sees Mike climbing down onto the tracks. She can see the headlights of the oncoming train.

She sprints. "Mike!" she screams. The few people on the platform step back in fear. The lights come relentlessly closer. Mike sees her and waves—he's still holding the Twinkie in one hand. Katie jumps down onto the track. She's met by the lights, the rumble, the wind.

"I have the answer, Mike!" she screams. "Don't do this!" She tries to pull him away.

"It's okay," he says peacefully. "I'm okay."

In the remaining moments before the collision, she tries to explain what she found when she reached the beginning of the Universe. The rumble of the train is too loud. Her pleading screams do not move him. She tugs at his arm; he tries to push her away. Two immovable forces. She can't leave him, and he won't move.

The pair of cold brown eyes watching them is weary, but filled with determination. Determination to not be a bystander, if only for this one moment. Thinking that, in what has been a year filled with trauma, loss, and sickness, they could and should try to help this lost soul.

Katie takes what she thinks might be her last moment alive to tell him, "Thank you, my friend. I love you." They both have tears in their eyes as the M train closes in.

The other people on the platform scream and wave their arms, trying in vain to warn the driver or stop the train. There's nothing they can do. The weathered metal car approaches unimpeded, its myriad metallic clatters reaching a crescendo.

The cold brown eyes are now on fire.

Onlookers see someone dive off the platform and collide with Mike and Katie, knocking them off-balance just as the train rages past.

It squeals and scrapes to a stop. The people on the platform step onto the train and race to get a look. There is nothing to see: no broken bones, no bodies, no bloody mess —just darkness.

The Answer

THE MANHATTAN-BOUND M train starts its way out of the station, clicking into the next section of the underground tunnel.

Huddled in a dugout between two iron girders in the tunnel wall are the three of them—terrified, but alive. "I think you're going to need this," the woman says, handing Mike his wallet back.

Katie's face, stained with tears, soot, and the accumulated dirt of the subway tunnels, manages to ask, "Are you one of us?"

The woman gives her a curious look. "We're all the same underneath, if that's what you mean, ma'am."

That isn't what Katie means.

She picks herself up from the black, powdery ground and looks into Mike's eyes. She sees true happiness for the first time.

"Thank you," Mike says.

"Do you need help? Are you all right?" the woman asks.

"I think I'm okay."

They climb to the platform and find their way back to the station entrance.

"Good luck," the woman says. They have reached her temporary encampment: her blanket, a rain jacket, and two shopping bags, neatly organized. "Maybe I'll see you again sometime."

"How about Wednesday, day after tomorrow, at eleven in the morning?"

"Sorry, what do you mean?"

Mike opens up his wallet and hands her a black business card with a blue circle on it.

"We have a vacancy at work, and you couldn't be more perfect for it," he says. "If you're looking for a job, that is."

* * *

At 10:55 a.m. on Wednesday, at an unremarkable building near 34th Street and 38th Avenue in Queens, the woman who, graciously and unrecognized, saved two lives the day before, walks past the nut vendor into the building's lobby. She examines the business card Mike had given her to confirm, *third floor*, as she enters the elevator.

Her name is Lita.

"Cream and sugar, right?" says Mike as he hands her a cup of coffee.

"Good guess."

"I'm an expert at guessing people's drinks. You should've seen me at the Christmas party."

He and Katie show Lita around the office. They talk about terms, salary, and perks.

"Subsidized housing... groceries delivered... transportation stipend... phone...."

They sit down and watch testimonial videos. The same

ones that Brooke showed to Katie at their first meeting in the office.

"Are those actors?" Lita asks.

"They're real," Katie says. "Can I show you one of yours?" Katie looks to Mike; they are in agreement. No secrets anymore.

"Okay."

They take Lita into the Archives. Mike asks her a few questions while Katie enters her answers into the query form on the old computer. Within a minute, Lita is in tears as she watches footage of herself: at age five making bread with her grandmother, learning to ride a bike with her father, playing with her brother who was stolen by leukemia twelve years ago, and the moment she decided to try to save Mike the day before.

"How do you know all these things?"

"We just know," says Katie.

Two days ago, Lita had been huddled in a subway station, invisible to the world. Hundreds of people walked past her everyday without a word. Each of them could see her, but for whatever kind of shame they felt, they would not look, or smile, or say hello.

She never asked for handouts. She was there for safety and shelter. She had nowhere to go and found ways to make it through the day, and the night. She collected forgotten clothes and discarded food. She used public restrooms and relocated regularly so as not to anger the authorities. And now, a gift. Just for being in the right place at the right time. *Incredible dumb luck*, she thinks.

"I want the job."

"Would you like to see your new place?" asks Mike. "Yours if you like it, that is."

"Yes, please." Lita nods; her heart skips a beat.

"Come on," he says with a gentle smile.

The three of them step through Frosted Glass Door Number 2, Mike's apartment. "Be sure you let the door close behind you," he says.

The moment the door closes, birdsong and breeze through the trees can be heard. Mike pushes through another door right in front of them into a studio apartment. Bright white walls, big windows, and a balcony overlooking the Hudson River.

Lita, her brown eyes brimming with tears, looks at the room, then to Mike and Katie. "Mine?" she asks, her voice barely a whisper.

"All yours. Have a look," he says.

Lita drifts around the apartment, opening cabinets and doors. She feels the cold granite countertop, the steel sink, the warm morning sun through the windows.

"It's beautiful," whispers Katie.

"It's whatever we want it to be."

Mike discovered this when Brooke told him in the early part of the twentieth century: *"I could have given you a view of Central Park or the fjords of Norway. But we must remain humble, and sacrificing your own happiness is worth it."*

Mike believed this for a long time. But now he knows it can be both. Even if life has some sweetness, problems can still be solved.

Lita admires the view—the river rippling by, a fisherman dropping a line.

"Move in anytime, start on Monday."

Lita nods, unable to speak without a flood of emotion.

"Does that work for you, Katie? Monday training?"

"Yes. Your first day will leave you breathless, Lita."

"Thank you," she says. "Thank you."

Mike leaves Lita with a few written instructions about coming and going and a couple of things to read over the next few days. Katie and Mike wish her well and say goodbye.

"What about your place?" Katie asks.

"I have a Plan B."

"Where will you live?"

"My name is on the title at 34 Commerce. Brooke won't need it anymore."

No, she won't. Katie had almost forgotten the first half of that day. Brooke is dead, Mike almost was... or could that have even happened?

From the moment Mike held any kind of consciousness, he'd wanted answers. His hunger to explore and his curiosity about the world was endless, but the answers he received only raised more questions. Transient life as an undercover agent, and being different from everyone he had ever met, left him hollow, hopeless, and alone.

"How do you feel?"

He has been asked this benign question before. For the first time, he has an honest answer.

"Free."

And he means it.

"Inside the Archives—how did you figure out the right question?" he asks.

"It's just something I always say under pressure. I'll show you."

The first elevator door slides open with a familiar creak. Mike presses the combination of buttons to enter the Archives.

On the screen, the cursor patiently flashes, waiting for a command. *It's always waiting*, Mike thinks. "Do your thing," he says. "I want to see this."

Katie nods, then types, WHAT THE FUCK IS THIS ALL ABOUT?

They share a smile, then she taps RETURN.

Mike watches the incredible show. Traveling through time and space, then climaxing in the immense display of the Big Bang.

Together they stand in the vast whiteness. There is nothing in any direction as far as the eye can see, except for one thing—a small, round glass table. It looks like something out of a French bistro. A sign is propped up on it.

They walk toward the table and then around to see what's on the sign. There are three words.

"It's really that simple, isn't it?"

"It should be."

The sign reads, *"Live, Laugh, Love."*

At that moment in her midsection, Katie feels a little kick.

Coda

SINCE MEETING with Brooke in Saint Malo, France a couple of centuries ago, they have kept an eye on things. They worked in the background—as tourists, waiters, public servants, window washers, and in countless other roles. They have nudged, influenced, and adjusted events to stop as much *veering off task* as they could.

"What will we do about the *dead husband*?" the round-faced woman with the long braid says in French.

"There are choices," says the slender, silver-haired man.

"You were good in the coffee shop. *More coffee for you two?*"

"I'm glad I can finally quit that job."

"Yes, the work is done—for now."

The wheels of change turn slowly. Actions have repercussions, and time can only go forward.

Corrections have to be made in the present and estimated for the future. The past is set.

They have been partners all along.

They stepped in for Katie on the day she went to the

movies. They executed satisfactory versions of her orders to help things *work themselves out*. This fractured her beliefs enough to break the rules in the Archives. They had maneuvered the unhoused woman to the subway. They knew Mike would use that entrance. He would be feeling hopeless for himself but still charitable and kind. That is who he is. He would help her, and she would save him. The power of seeing and being seen.

It turns out that Brooke was right in saying someone would save him.

The cone diagram they looked at showed that those actions would lead to a new employee, a replacement for Brooke.

"It took four centuries to set this right," the man says in French, relief in his voice.

"And the next four centuries will be the beneficiary," the woman answers.

He sits next to her in front of the hologram—it rests on a frozen frame of a cityscape.

There will be a new set of problems soon, and a well-earned day of rest tomorrow, but a job well done is a job well done. It is time for a celebration. A cork pulls from a bottle of wine—a Bordeaux from 1965.

They toast.

"Santé."

"Encore une fois, s'il te plaît?" she asks with a smile.

"Of course, one more time—it is so good."

The frozen hologram starts to play. A woman's voice screams, "Katie, I DON'T WANT TO DIE!" Someone runs past the view, revealing a large, boxy delivery truck. A moment later, the truck swerves, nearly missing a taxi. The taxi, desperate to avoid a collision, brakes, spins out of control, and careens into a metal streetlight pole. The pole jerks violently in response. An electrical wire yanks free from the pole with a sharp crackle. Gravity pulls the wire toward the earth, and it lands in a puddle of rainwater. A blinding spark flashes, and a scream is cut short.

The last ten seconds of Brooke's life.

Acknowledgments

The Universe formed in the cramped bathroom of a penthouse apartment near downtown Los Angeles. A book of motivational ideas and quotes, left open on the west-facing windowsill, featured a page about *putting things out to the Universe.*

Clearly, the Universe wanted me to find that book in the bathroom and start telling its story—so I took the job.

Thank you, Katherine Takahashi, for your perfectly placed reading materials and incredible support throughout this process. The main character is named for you. Thank you to my old friend Rob Gibbs for hearing my early pitch of The Universe, bouncing ideas around, and getting on board with developing the screenplay based on this book. We may still be working on it as you read this.

Eternal gratitude to Jamila Koch for her brilliant artwork throughout the book. You can find her @jammiekoko on Instagram. For their sharp notes and steady support—thank you, in no particular order: Sherry Matzdorff (my dear mother), Eve Connell, Brooke Adams, Stephen Boucher, Nina Colman, and Tony Shalhoub.

For guidance with the German language bits, thanks to Thor Freudenthal. The French language bits, thanks to Tim

Lind, Luc Mena, and Adrien Pladys. The Spanish language bits, thanks to Beatriz Yanovich, Maria Montoreano and Alberto Plasencia Gonzalez. For help with Cone Diagram design, Scott Gordon at HaloLA.tv.

To the good folks at the Coffee Commissary and Three Sisters, my "offices" for much of the writing of this book, thank you for the endless coffee and free Wi-Fi.

The character of *Katie* was influenced by the real-life Katie Aselton, who once saved my butt on a film set.

Cover design: Me & Katherine Takahashi
Cover illustration: Me
Other, far better, illustrations: Jamila Koch

About the Author

Mike Matzdorff is a father of two, a midwesterner, is still searching for the perfect acoustic guitar, and delights in storytelling.

Find him on Substack, or other social media, @mikematzdorff.